WITHDRAW

D0830075

ADVANCE PRAISE FOR

"*The Swells* is a brilliantly acerbic upstairs-downstairs satire of class and privilege on the high seas. Will Aitken is a singular voice in our literary landscape." —JORDAN TANNAHILL, author of Scotiabank Giller Prize finalist *The Listeners*

"Careful not to spill that flute of Veuve Clicquot on your Jimmy Choos as you're swept away on the waves of this riotous high-seas satire where the 1 percent become the 99. The delectable queer love child of *Condé Nast Traveller*, *The Great Gatsby*, Karl Marx, and P. G. Wodehouse, *The Swells* asks if revolution is like rearranging diamonds and deckchairs on the Titanic, if utopia is the worst form of society except for all the others. Strap on your Mae West: this voyage is an archly, artfully, uproariously breezy yet incisive dark delight." —GARY BARWIN, author of Scotiabank Giller Prize finalist *Yiddish for Pirates* and *Nothing the Same, Everything Haunted*

"In *The Swells*, Will Aitken's brilliant new novel, the most luxurious cruise ship on the seas floats right-side up, but the passengers and crew are turned upside down. On board, a class mutiny yields an eviscerating yet hilarious reversal of fortunes and a stinging, darkly veiled satire that left me laughing and thinking long after I turned the last page." —TERRY FALLIS, two-time winner of the Stephen Leacock Medal for Humour

SEP 0 7 2022

Also by the Author

Fiction

Terre Haute

A Visit Home

Realia

Non-Fiction

Death in Venice: A Queer Film Classic

*Antigone Undone: Juliette Binoche, Anne Carson,
Ivo van Hove, and the Art of Resistance*

The Swells

WILL AITKEN

ANANSI

WHITCHURCH-STOUFFVILLE PUBLIC LIBRARY

Copyright © 2022 Will Aitken

Published in Canada in 2022 and the USA in 2022 by House of Anansi Press Inc.
www.houseofanansi.com

All rights reserved. No part of this publication may be reproduced or transmitted in
any form or by any means, electronic or mechanical, including photocopying, record-
ing, or any information storage and retrieval system, without permission in writing
from the publisher.

House of Anansi Press is committed to protecting our natural environment. This book
is made of material from well-managed FSC®-certified forests, recycled materials, and
other controlled sources.

House of Anansi Press is a Global Certified Accessible™ (GCA by Benetech) publisher.
The ebook version of this book meets stringent accessibility standards and is available to students and readers with print disabilities.

26 25 24 23 22   1 2 3 4 5

Library and Archives Canada Cataloguing in Publication

Title: The swells / Will Aitken.
Names: Aitken, Will, 1949- author.
Identifiers: Canadiana (print) 20210285141 | Canadiana (ebook) 202102851\5X |
ISBN 9781487009694
  (softcover) | ISBN 9781487009700 (EPUB)
Classification: LCC PS8551.I78 S94 2022 | DDC C813/.54—dc23

Book design: Alysia Shewchuk

*House of Anansi Press respectfully acknowledges that the land on which we operate is the
Traditional Territory of many Nations, including the Anishinabeg, the Wendat, and the
Haudenosaunee. It is also the Treaty Lands of the Mississaugas of the Credit.*

With the participation of the Government of Canada
Avec la participation du gouvernement du Canada | Canadä

*We acknowledge for their financial support of our publishing program the Canada Council
for the Arts, the Ontario Arts Council, and the Government of Canada.*

Printed and bound in Canada

For my dear pod, Sora Olah and Mike Tyrell,
and for my mother, Helen Armstrong Aitken.

At sea a fellow comes out.
Salt water is like wine, in that respect.

—HERMAN MELVILLE
LETTER TO EVERT DUYCKINCK, 1857

1

THE GIANT MANTA RAY's shadow wafts across Briony's menu as she sits alone at a table for two in the *Entre deux eaux* brasserie, a new seven-star underwater restaurant with sheer glass walls.

She's awaiting her main course — the lettuce gazpacho with brown crab and whey granita starter had been less than supernal — when her phone rings. Actually *rings*.

What a catastrophe! She's forgotten to turn it off, it rings so rarely. The first "Yeh-ay" of Tierra Whack's "Only Child" ripples across the dining room to the dismay of all. She sees the *maître d*'s head bob up before she succeeds in muting the ring tone. "Sorry," she mouths to him, but he's already turned away in disdain.

She knows who's calling without even checking the display: Gemma! the only person she knows who still uses her phone for talking. Gemma! editor-in-chief of world-renowned *Euphoria!* magazine, where Briony's employed as Luxury Travel Associate Editor. Gemma! whose lithium's always going wonky. Gemma! sixty if she's a day.

"Briony, Briony, Briony! Where *are* you when I need you most?"

She tells her even though Gemma knows perfectly well.

"So much has happened here — volcanic! — you won't believe."

"Oh?"

"Amazing news, and I wanted you to be the first to know — why I'm reaching out to you."

Briony tenses. Last time Gemma reached out she got slapped. Figuratively.

"Can you guess?"

"No."

"The most wonderful thing."

"Yes?"

"We've been sold!"

"Sold what?"

"*Euphoria!*'s been sold, you old silly."

"Oh?"

"I told you we were looking for a buyer."

"No."

"I'm certain I did. But it's been such an absolute flurry here I don't know what I've babbled to whom. You remember the Macau twins?"

"The macaw twins? *Birds,* Gemma?"

"*Macau.* China, casinos, fabulously wealthy twins — so young! so sleek! so sharky! — looking to diversify their... their *holdings* and —"

"Launder their money?"

"Briony, you are such a card! Their offer, substantial if not quite generous — hard-headed, these boys — gives us a fresh new leash on life —"

"Lease?" Briony offers.

"No, same lease. No one's talking about our lease, Briony. Listen up! The lease remains the same... for now. But *Euphoria!*, our dear old glossy *Euphoria!*, is no more."

"No?"

"Long live the new *Euphoria!* We're going online."

"We're already online," Briony says.

"Yes, yes, of course we are. Everyone knows that. But the old, the old—what do you call it?—non-digital, old *monaural* bits of the magazine—"

"Analog?"

"*Analog.* Why I keep you around, good girl with the right word at the right—The analog bits are no more, the print issue dead as a doorknob."

"Mouse?"

"Who mentioned mice? Certainly not I."

"Not at all, no."

"All this will, as you can imagine, entail some right-sizing in various departments. Dear plus-size Rayon in Style Supreme!—gone! Deandra in, er, Street Meats! was it?—gone!"

"Street Smarts?"

"And poor little Perry in Local Colour!—love him to bits—how does he get his hair to do that?—but the concept never really soared, did you think? Or did you?"

Briony's too busy contemplating her own probable demise to answer.

"But you, you, you, Briony, you are moving up and out."

Up she likes, *out*—ouf. "Yes, Gemma?"

"The whole luxury-travel section—what's it called?"

"*Voyageur!*"

"Is over, *qua* section. Long reads as well—gone. Too slow. Boggy. Freelancers—over! Too dear. But just think: *Jaunt!* will be all Briony all the way."

"*Jaunt?*"

"Briony, I can hear the skepticism in your voice, but '*Voyageur!*' sounded too foreign, '*Vagabond!*' too passé, and '*Traipse!*' far too rustic, while '*Jaunt!*' has that slight retro touch I adore, that cabriolet-with-wicker-picnic-basket-packed-with-Spode-in-the-boot cachet — so ineffably right!"

"Mmm."

"And it will be entirely your turf to manage as you please."

"What about Annabella?"

"Gone gone gone! I *hated* having to call security to escort her from the building. *Not* a good sport."

"No?"

"With her out of the picture, you choose the topics, you do all the travel, you write all the copy. Well, less space as I indicated earlier, but all for you."

"I see."

"I expected more enthusiasm, Briony. More brio! Can't you see how this will free you up? You'll still be on contract, *ça va sans dire*, but like everyone else at your level — everyone who didn't get the chop — your position will be unruminative."

"Unremunerated?"

"Bingo! So right! You will quite naturally retain all your travel perks — unlimited free jaunting for Briony girl — and will be responsible for one piece per month — 500-word max and most preferable as listicle — for which *Euphoria!* will pay $200 USD, plus $75 for each photo, up to a limit of two. Of course we won't need photos for this trip — we'll snatch them off the webernet."

"Yes?"

"You will also retain your membership at the *Euphoria!* Supper Club and Spa, here for you to use whenever you're in Manhattan. We've waived the yearly dues for you — just because you *are* you — and a select few others, so you will pay only a token user's fee each visit."

"Right."

"You see now, Briony, how everything changes and yet nothing really changes at all? You remain a cherished member of the *Euphoria!* family and begin this terrific new adventure with us with fewer responsibilities and more time — oodles, just oodles of it! — to explore and write and generally jaunt about. Think of the freedom this entails, the opportunities that will open up before you. Now is the right time to prioritize your future! When you're back from —"

Briony tells Gemma her present location once more.

"Yes, yes. When you're back, do drop by my office so we can wrinkle out the details of —"

"Uh, winkle?"

"Honestly, Briony, why would you bring up molluscs as a time like —"

Briony blows into her phone, taps it twice with her fork and cries, "You're breaking up, Ge —"

She ends the call, opens the FlipItFast app. A few deft keystrokes and her Park Slope–adjacent studio's on the market — furnished! She leaves her table just as the server brings in her John Dory smothered in nettles, radishes, and squid ink. Who has time to eat? She must pack.

This is how Briony's life of sumptuous new homelessness begins. She will now travel from gig to luxury travel gig, with only the designer togs in her luggage, paying nothing, earning less, and never ever really setting down.

NEXT MORNING SHE WHISKS out the revolving door — the tropical sun nails her to the Royal Morningwood Hotel's scarlet runner.

Mimi, the *Emerald Tranquility*'s PR flack, calls up from the open limo door: "Hurry, Briony, we're going to be late."

Descending the wide marble stairs, Briony senses a stirring in the topiaries. "Careful, Miss!" the greatcoated doorman calls out. In a burst of blue-black hair and sparkling teeth, a street kid leaps out of the topiaries and bounds toward her, palm already outstretched. Briony's about to give him her last few *palagosi* when the doorman pulls a wooden cosh from the inside pocket of his coat and clubs the boy mid-flight. Whoosh and soar crumple into rags, ribs, and tarry feet. The blood haloing his head darkens the runner from scarlet to aubergine.

Briony makes to go to the boy, but the doorman clasps her elbow and propels her down the stairs and into the limo back seat, crushing Mimi against Gigot, the new young travel journalist from Paris, who's pressed up against the tinted window, bronzer running.

"That was close," Mimi says.

"We can't just go." Briony tries to re-open her door but the driver has locked them in. "Open this door!"

"Calm down, Briony." Mimi touches her shoulder. "You know better than to interfere in a local problem."

"We have to help him!"

Mimi looks at her doubtfully. "This isn't at all like you."

Gigot bestirs. "He will be all fine?"

"He's badly hurt." Briony looks out the window.

"Only unconscious," Mimi notes. The limo begins to pull away.

A phalanx of gardeners in picturesque conical hats advances through the topiaries. They lift the boy-shaped limpness and carry him not into the Royal Morningwood's marbled lobby but down a nearby bleak laneway.

"Where are they taking him?" Briony asks, frantic.

"To a small free clinic run by nuns, probably." Mimi rummages in her tote.

"He will not die?" Gigot says, his face gone ashen.

Mimi pats his tremulous hand. "Street kids — tough as old boots." She taps out two gold capsules into his palm. "You poor kid. Hold these under your tongue till they dissolve."

"We have to go back!"

"You should have a couple of these too, Briony."

"The poor homeless kid," Briony cries.

Mimi looks her in the eye. "I'd never have taken you for a sentimentalist."

.   .   .

GOLD STAFF-PASS FLASHING, Mimi ushers them through Her Imperial Majesty's Royal Embarkation Hall and Eco Centre, a semi-conscious Gigot softly raving. Past regular passengers with fortresses of leather luggage stacked round their ankles, past guards brandishing assault rifles, past veiled women waving drug wands over passengers' bodies.

The jolly customs officer holds out a crystal bowl: "Please take mint."

He stamps Mimi's American and Gigot's French passports but pauses to study Briony's navy blue one.

"Canada!" he cries, "Dancing friend to the free world!"

Mimi and Briony propel Gigot up the gangway. The *Emerald Tranquility*'s Atrium Lobby opens out before them — hectares of ormolu, gold fringe, bevelled mirrors, linenfold wainscotting, plushy Aubussons. Up on the mezzanine, an old man in a paisley bow tie plinks out "Slow Boat to China" on the glass grand piano.

And everywhere the very aged perambulate, white-uniformed attendants following closely.

"I may not have mentioned," Mimi says to Briony, "the *Emerald Tranquility* appeals to a slightly older demographic."

A veteran of many cruises, Briony knows this — the pricier the ship, the older the clientele. She knows as well the *Emerald Tranquility*'s the richest ship afloat. "Lot of burials at sea?"

Mimi giggles. "If only that were allowed. You can't imagine the freezer space they take up."

A gong sounds at the top of the curving glass staircase.

A small golden boy in a saffron robe cries out, "All hail His Great Holy Abundance, Little Butter!"

A dozen similarly clad boys descend, waving joss sticks, clacking finger cymbals.

A bald man of indeterminate age bowls forward, golden as the boys but less lissome, saffron robe draped to reveal one podgy shoulder.

"Who the hell is Little Butter?" Briony asks too loudly.

"Little Butter?" Mimi looks confused. "Oh Briony, Little Buddha!"

"He's a real Buddha?"

"He's cagey about that. His real name's something else. Honestly, my memory . . . freezer time for old Mimi. Sounds like 'shrimp cocktail.' He claims his followers insist on calling him Buddha — oh yes, Praun Thalat."

He floats down the stairs as the golden boys weave in and out of his ambit, cymbals stuttering faster now, incense smoke billowing.

"Little Buddha!" an ancient woman in an electric wheelchair calls out. Her coterie take it up. "Little Buddha!" an old fellow in an embroidered silk dressing gown cries. "Little Buddha!" a woman wearing a fingertip veil over ivory sunglasses sighs.

Briony assumes he's headed toward his adherents, but he plants himself directly before her and smiles a golden smile.

"What does he want?" Briony whispers to Mimi.

A golden boy steps forward, a gilt cage dangling from his forefinger. "His Great Holy Abundance would present you with this small token of his esteem."

Briony sticks out her finger, and the boy loops the gold cord over it. A scuttle and whirr within. Through the bars she makes out a live cricket: iridescent wing shields, flying buttress legs.

"It is a sign," the golden boy announces, "of plentiful squid and related fecundity."

Briony smiles down at Little Buddha. "Please thank His Great Holy Abundance for me."

Little Buddha whispers to the boy.

"His Great Holy Abundance would also like to bestow on you the Kiss of Peace."

This sets the old people behind her aflutter: "He's granting *her* the Kiss of Peace?" "What has she done to deserve the goddamn Kiss of Peace?"

Little Buddha stands on tiptoe. Puckering lips zoom in on Briony's.

He cries out, a drop of blood depends from his second chin. Briony steps back, wipes a hand across her mouth. Not the Kiss of Peace but Kiss of Tongue.

2

LOUIS ARMSTRONG'S CRUSTY VOICE fills Briony's penthouse suite. "'Sail away, sail away/We will cross the mighty waters—'" Then, "'Sail away, sail away/We will cross—'"

What happened to the rest? "'Sail away , sail away/We will cross—'"

They've looped it!

The casting-off whump of the *Emerald Tranquility*'s ship horn vibrates her veneers.

"'Sail away—'"

Thuds at the massive mahogany door. She hauls it open. Gigot tumbles in.

"'Sail away—'"

Whump! Whump!

"Briony, what is this most terrible sound?"

"It's the ship's horn, Gigot. It means we're casting off."

"*Mais non.* I know the sound of the ship horn. I am not so inexperience I have not cruised before. But what is this voice that sounds like *le gargarisme?*"

"Gargling?"

"'We will cross the mighty—'"

"Please make it stop."

"It's the *Emerald Tranquility*'s signature tune. Louis Armstrong. Before your time. Before mine for that matter. You'll be hearing it a lot."

"So disturbing. Like this old man who chokes on his own *flegme*. This is an English word?"

"Unfortunately. Come on, time to go up on Wraith Deck for the casting-off party."

"All I desire is to return to my room for a small siesta." For the first time Gigot takes in the sleek Italian minimalism of Briony's suite and the wide veranda where the torpid sea makes its first slide-by. She suspects that down on Zircon Deck he's got a Juliet balcony he can't step out on, a bathroom he can't turn around in, and a Farrow & Ball accent wall. "Your place is such huge!"

"We better get going."

He holds up his phone. "No one will object if I take photos and the little videos too?"

"Just don't let anyone know you're a journo. Didn't Mimi explain?"

"Mimi explains so much all the time."

"It's a long cruise — get used to it."

"I will try my most."

"The important thing to remember is we're strictly incognito. The punters must never know we're travelling for free."

His eyes light up. "There's a footy team onboard?"

"Sorry, no. Punters are paying guests."

"It is all so confusing. At CELSA they told us —"

"SALSA?"

"*L'École des hautes études en sciences de l'information et de la communication,* at the Sorbonne?"

"You actually have a journalism degree?"

He shakes his head. "Communication Studies."

Briony chokes on her own laughter.

"Something is wrong?" Gigot asks.

"Nothing. Nothing. I've just never met a live one before."

MIMI SURGES ACROSS WRAITH DECK. "Where have you been? At least you got here in time for *Kimi Ga Yo!*"

"We're having Korean?"

"Someone hasn't been reading her electronic press kit. *Kimi Ga Yo* is Japan's national anthem."

"We are sailing to Japan?" Gigot says. He's already fixated, Briony notices, on the servers in black-tie and bum jackets who waltz across Wraith Deck balancing salvers set with champagne flutes.

Mimi pats his cheek. "You haven't done your reading either, naughty boy. The *Emerald Tranquility*, like its sister ship the *Jade Nirvana*, is Japanese-owned."

Four Japanese girls in white lace everything stroll out on deck. As the Rising Sun ascends the flagpole, they saw away on tiny Suzukis. A canned male voice sings in Japanese over the ship loudspeaker.

"That was fast," Briony whispers to Mimi.

"Shortest national anthem in the world."

The girls take it from the top again, this time singing the English translation:

May your reign continue
Continue for a thousand, eight thousand generations
Until the pebbles
Grow to boulders.

A smattering of polite applause for this imperfect grasp of geology. "There's our captain now," Mimi says as a bearded behemoth in a gold-piped uniform lumbers past. "Let me introduce you."

Briony grabs two flutes of champagne, downs one, hands the other to Gigot, and snatches a third for herself. Mimi has disappeared in the crush.

"Aren't you starving?" Briony steers Gigot toward the buffet, where white tablecloths snap in the wind. The ship takes a deep roll. From the wheelchair squadron parked near the elevators, a chair slips its moorings and careens toward the string quartet, who scamper away winningly. The woman in the speeding chair, bouffant comb-out gone vertical, bounces off the starboard rail, knocks the stick-food table off-kilter, and slams into the captain's knees.

He's down.

A dozen servers point black Micro-Uzis at wheelchair lady's head.

From a prone position the captain shouts, "Stand down, Gummis!"

It takes three of them to haul him to his feet while the rest tower menacingly over wheelchair lady.

"Gummis!"

They lower their weapons with some reluctance. Upright once more, the captain breaks through their bristling semicircle. "My dear Madame Flocon-d'Hiver! You must forgive my Gummis. They are always a bit trigger-happy until we're well away from port."

Madame Flocon-d'Hiver has regained her dignity, if not her coiffure. "Captain, it's marvellous to see how alert your boys are. I shall sleep more soundly tonight in that knowledge."

One of the tamer Gummis bows, steps back, and clicks his heels. Gigot steps forward to offer his barely touched champagne to the shaken woman.

"There you are!" Mimi rushes forward. "Wasn't that exciting?"

"Gummis, Mimi?" Briony asks.

"Short for *Gummibärchen*, darling. You know: Gummi Bears. Captain thought we needed a non-threatening name for ship security."

Gigot quivers. "They give me such a *frisson emotionelle*."

A gong sounds on high. Little Buddha stands on the poop deck encircled by his minions.

With Madame Flocon-d'Hiver wheeled away and the Micro-Uzis re-concealed, the casting-off party has once more taken on a festive tone. A man with Mick Jagger's lips and nothing else steals the sushi chef's blue-and-white bandana and brandishes it like an abbreviated bullfighter's cape. A Suzuki girl charges, thrusting forth lacy forefinger horns.

Little Buddha indicates the gong boy should strike more forcefully — the kid knocks it out of the park. Everyone turns to stare.

"Silence!" Little Buddha commands. "Captain Kartoffeln has asked me to say a few brief words as we venture forth on this magical journey."

A tall blonde in a silvery sheath touches one ruby earring as her portly companion checks his mobile, only to discover the ship has already sailed beyond reception.

"We are usually insulated from the world and its clamours," Little Buddha says. "But even on a voyage wholly dedicated to pleasure and escape, we nevertheless must face facts.

"Our rivers are burbling sewers, our oceans putridly moribund, our air gristly and unbreathable, our political systems farcically redundant. We think our privilege and pelf will protect us from global annihilation. And so they will, my dears. But only to a point."

Briony assumes his jeremiad will put people off. Instead they draw nearer, full of anticipatory anguish.

"The world drowns in excrement, but you have climbed to the highest peak and down you look, thinking, 'Nothing can touch me here.' You imagine you will survive but you cannot forever, dear ones, for even now the world into a stinking charnel house is turning."

"So true," a gangly man in a midnight-blue tuxedo mutters.

"You must ask yourselves now: who will save me from the shit?"

A woman in a tartan romper pleads, "Who will save us, Little Buddha? Who?"

"Only you can yourself save you, madame. Abandon your profligate ways! Only love, compassion, and true-heartedness can help you now. Only renunciation of your past greedy ways will transform you."

"But what can we do, Little Buddha?" a stooped man in black-tie and red lizard cowboy boots wonders aloud. "How may we help?"

"I am so glad you have asked this most important question, fine gentleman."

Golden boys fan out through the crowd carrying digital card readers. "Along with countless million others, you too may give generously to our New Harmony Foundation Ltd. Your American dollars, your pesos and euros, your yen and baht, even your pathetic post-Brexit pounds sterling will all go toward our magnanimous and urgent crusade to save the world before it is too late, before your own dear mouths are crammed with sewage, your ears most foully stopped and your eyes seeing only brown."

Briony watches as men remove flashing timepieces and drop them into the boys' small hands. A stately woman in ruched lavender organza unfastens her plum-diamond choker and hands it to an approving golden boy. Another boy politely refuses a hyper-tanned young woman's earrings, murmuring, "No seed pearls, please."

3

TROPICAL SUNSETS, BRIONY THINKS — why do they even bother? Pink skid marks, mauve striations in the west, and the day hurtles down into black. In the instant between oblivion and the fairy lights twinkling up across Wraith Deck, she stares over the rail as the ship's phosphorescent wake flares out from its steep flank, an incandescent invitation to race out onto the flat black sea. Always such a comforting thought for her, this idea of permanent release.

"Briony! Don't you dare!"

She spins around. "Terence? Terence Tri?"

"Teenah Tri now."

They're in each other's arms though neither has appeared to move, borne on a symbiotic rush sharper than riptide.

A thousand questions arise, none Briony cares to ask. Plenty of time, she reflects, to throw herself seaward with no regrets when Teenah has disappeared once more, vanishing her greatest talent.

THEY CLATTER DOWN A metal companionway to Chopard Deck and race along the deep-pile corridor. Heaving open the door to her suite, Briony propels an unresisting Teenah through the dark.

The flow's instantaneous—all the old conjugations rediscovered, deepened.

Yet everything's new: Teenah's freshly minted, and Briony's moved by her compliance as together they swim the damp linens. Near the end Teenah surprises her once more when she uses Briony's lips for rich sport.

How can we be so practised and still so headlong spontaneous? Briony asks herself as Teenah finally falls away from her. Her mouth unstopped, Briony howls.

WHEN SHE AWAKENS, Teenah's dressed. "Must you go?"

"What kind of question's that?"

"Come back to bed."

"Seriously?"

"Don't you dare laugh at me."

"Briony, this is so not you."

"What's that supposed to mean?"

"When have you ever wanted me to stay?"

"Lots of times."

"Yeah, right. Once you come you always long for me to go."

"That's not what I want tonight."

"This is so fucking weird."

"But we haven't seen each other in eons."

Teenah sits down on the bed and takes Briony's hand. "You know that's not true. It's only been two years since we were in Cinque Terra—remember how you tried to push that hedge-fund turd off the Blue Path?"

"That was five years ago."

"No way."

"Way."

"But what about that night in the Sierra Mixtecas with all the peyote buttons and you wanted to adopt the three-legged feral cat? That can't have been more than three years ago."

"Wasn't me — you know how I hate cats."

Teenah tries to furrow her brow. "Oh, right. Must have been Francesca. Or maybe Phineas?"

"We *never* see each other, and now you want to eat and run."

"I have other obligations."

"Fine."

"Oh, please."

"What?"

"The Briony I know was never a pouter." Teenah lets go of her hand and stands. "And what was with that sound you made?"

"Sound?"

"There at the end — really loud."

"I've always been a shouter."

"It was more like someone in deep distress."

"Don't be absurd."

"It's not like you won't see me again — I'm stuck on this fucking boat, same as you."

Teenah's out the door. Briony falls back against crushed pillows feeling wretched and abandoned. She wills herself back into unconsciousness.

.   .   .

ALONE IN THE RAVAGED BED, she had anticipated a sleepless night of tossing self-recrimination, but her sleep's fathomless, end-stopped by a dream of large rats pouring out of small teacups. The titanium grandfather clock chimes seven. She realizes she can just make it to Second Seating. The hunger! She stares at her mucilaginous chin in the bathroom's bronze-tinted mirror. When she points the remote at the alabaster sarcophagus, it glows as water gushes in.

As she's slipping into her robe, Collins the Butler bustles in, arms overladen with muslin-draped evening gowns.

"These have been lightly steamed with the faintest mist of Malaysian highland panic-grass, miss."

"So thoughtful of you, Collins."

"Will you allow me to bring you a champagne and caviar before-dinner snack?"

"Is there time?"

"Always time for champagne and caviar, miss."

"Perhaps not — I have to do my face."

"A spot of nothing just there, miss." With a fragrant cloth he scours her still-sticky chin. "I will be delighted to help with your face."

"You can do that?"

"Indeed, miss. I don't usually mention it as it's not among our proffered services, but it's rare I'm allowed to attend to a face as young and lovely as yours."

He disappears into the bedroom, returns with a transparent apron over his buttling rig, and applies himself to her face.

"Collins?"

"Yes, miss?"

"Could we dispense with 'miss,' if only between these walls? Sounds too much like cosplay."

"What would miss prefer to be called?"

"Briony."

"It would be a pleasure, Miss Briony."

She feels subtly baited. He slaps on concealer with a dab hand.

"What's your real name, Collins?"

"Luis."

"Where are you from, Luis?"

"Colombia."

"And your fake plummy accent comes from where?"

"London. Berlitz International, Kensington High Street."

"How do you sound after a few drinks?"

"Ay, caramba!" He bats his eyelashes.

"You do other stereotypes as well?"

"Before I went to study to become a butler, I majored in performance art and digital branding at Universidad Nacional de Colombia. I am proficient in Agricultural *Campesino,* Simple Careworn Urban *Madre,* Pederastic Catholic Cardinal, Pouty Cantina Vamp—"

"With your many talents it must be boring for you aboard the *Emerald Tranquility.*"

"The money's not bad, compared to home. I send most of it back to my widowed *mamacita* so she can better care for my seven brothers and sisters and the little blind autistic girl we took in after the tsunami."

"Seriously, Luis?"

"I am but one child. It all goes to my *puta* of a boyfriend so we can buy an ocean-view condo in a gated compound."

"How's that going for you?"

"It all goes up *la puta's* nose."

"Surely not."

"I am an artist — where would I be without hyperbole? We must do something for this hair too, once I finish threading your eyebrows. My mother has a little three-basin salon in the *barrio*."

"Really?"

"Briony, soon you'll know all my little ways and there will be no more mystery. My mother's a copy writer at Ogilvy & Mather's Bogotá office."

BRIONY WATCHES A SILENT couple dine alone at a small table near the kitchen, thinking there's always a sad dyad like theirs on every cruise: he in business formal, she in a tarnished sequin cocktail dress. They have nothing to say to each other, basilisk stare meeting basilisk stare, though instant death smites neither, only life-in-death at a table for two.

Perhaps they are not unhappy? Do they commune spiritually with no words needed? With a practised hand he reaches out and cuffs her. Her head bounces off the veloured wall — a brief stunned look. He signals the waiter for another drink. She goes back to picking at her Cobb salad.

"Mimi, did you see that?"

Mimi's midstream in a monologue explaining the dining room's social hierarchy as Gigot's exquisite cleft chin subsides toward the napery.

"Mimi!"

"Briony, please. Can't you see I'm —"

"That man over there — he just hit his wife."

She cranes her neck. "The one in the off-the-rack suit? Oh, surely not. They look like a perfectly respectable couple. A tad underdressed for the occasion, but one can see they've made an effort."

"He socked her, Mimi."

She shakes her head. "That sort of thing simply does not happen on a ship of this calibre. That's the kind of behaviour one would expect on Viking or" — she shudders — "Carnival. *Emerald Tranquility* passengers are people of breeding and discernment who would never conduct themselves in a vulgar way."

Briony pushes back her chair. "I'm getting the *maître d'*."

Mimi pins Briony's wrist to the cool damask. "You will do nothing of the sort. Whatever you think you saw is a personal matter between husband and wife."

"It's assault. It happened in a public place. I'm sure I'm not the only witness."

"You can't know that."

The shaken woman stands up, livid and confused. Savouring his drink, the man ignores her. Briony attempts to stand as well.

"If you leave this table," Mimi hisses, pulling her back down, "you will never sail with the *Emerald Tranquility* again."

"You didn't see what he did."

"How do you know if you even saw what you think you saw? You've been drinking pretty steadily since you got here."

"I don't call three glasses of champagne steady drinking. I am soberly perfect."

For the first time Gigot notices Mimi has Briony's hand clamped to the table.

"But Mimi, you are hurting Briony."

"Stay out of this, Gigot."

Unaccustomed to sharp speaking, he crimsons.

"Mimi!" Briony barks in the older woman's face. Mimi starts back, loosening her grip, and Briony stands. People at nearby tables turn to stare. A lady at the nearest table lobs a bun that bounces off Gigot's cheek.

Briony tears away. The punched woman's dress glitters forlornly in the distance. Scores of ball gowns and twice that many servers impede Briony's progress. The assaulted woman staggers out the door as Teenah makes her own sparkling entrance in couture so bare it's more a rumour of a gown than a proper dress.

Briony knows she should run after the poor woman, but Teenah's nearly unclad presence makes her reformulate her position. Let heteronormativity hash out its own stale problems, she thinks, as she takes Teenah in her arms.

4

NEXT MORNING THE *Emerald Tranquility* arrives at Randarum, its first port of call. Ecstatic at the prospect of getting off the ship, Briony rises at dawn to watch land's slow approach. Luis sets out breakfast for one on the balcony. Teenah had returned to her suite shortly before dawn, leaving Briony with a tousled bed and a sore throat. Luis lays out two sets of tongs — one for sugar, the other for lemon slices. She murmurs to herself, "'My home away from home is better than home.'" Not hard to achieve, she tells herself, when you no longer have a home.

"Sorry, Briony?"

"Page one of the electronic press kit."

"I see."

"Luis, have you visited Randarum before?"

He pours her coffee. "You know, first time I'm on this ship, every port of call I am there — exploring, visiting museums and historical sites, buying gifts for all my brothers and sisters back home."

"Didn't you say you're an only child?"

"It is so hard, Briony, to serve you the authenticity you desire. To tell you the truth, though we have sailed to Randarum many times, I have never bothered to go ashore. Port calls are always the same. You will be escorted every moment while off the boat — a small problem with the

religious minority in the south — so you will see and do
the normal things rich people see and do in Asian ports."

"What do these religious people do?"

"Mass electrocutions."

"Really?"

"Stay with the group, my dear Briony."

SHE WATCHES FROM THE taffrail as Randarum's renowned
red beaches heave into view. After a mammoth chemical
spill in the late '90s, the island decided to ride with it rather
than pay for an expensive eco-scouring. She can make out
wooden shanties with blue tile roofs and clouds of yellow
gardenia rioting everywhere.

As the *Emerald Tranquility* coaches leave the beach,
Briony glimpses a municipal sign:

SWIMMING FORBIDDEN HERE

PLEASE LIMIT STROLLS TO 7 MINUTES

FOLLOWED BY COMPULSORY FOOTBATH

They drive an eighth of a kilometre inland, wheezing
to a halt in a public square bordered by brick godowns
in faded gold, blue, and pink, with turquoise doors and
window frames with yellow shutters.

Mimi surges about waving a green pennant emblazoned with a pair of kissing seahorses — the *Emerald
Tranquility*'s logo — picked out in pearls and tourmalines.

"Welcome to Randarum," Mimi bleats through a small
bullhorn. "What a treat to visit this colourful and historic

island, at one time a bustling port where merchants vied to buy and sell silk, coffee, tea, spices, and the highly coveted blue marble once found in inland quarries.

"More recently Randarum has become a burgeoning high-tech locus where armies of tireless young girls assemble smart TVs for our viewing pleasure.

"We've alighted in the oldest part of the city, formerly known as Coolies' End and more recently renamed the Old Quarter. The multihued godowns, or warehouses, are perfect replicas of the originals destroyed in the Three-Day War of 1987 with neighbouring Santorum. They now house not fragrant spices or pearly rice but rather Prada, Burberry, Bottega Veneta, and all the other international luxury brands we never tire of delighting in as we cruise and shop from port to exotic port."

A small golden boy tugs at the skirt of Mimi's sundress. She tilts her head as he whispers in her ear.

"I don't think we'll have time, sweetheart." She gently shoves the boy away.

Little Buddha steps forth. "It would be a dirty shame if we did not visit one of Randarum's holiest temples — the legendary Mirror Wat."

Mimi lowers the bullhorn, but snatches of their conversation carry on the fetid breeze: "Impossible — The loveliest — My tour not yours — Not to be missed — No time — Not so far — Not on your life — Small token of my —" Mimi slips Little Buddha's small gold envelope into her sundress pocket.

"Ladies and gentlemen, Little Buddha informs me we are but steps away from one of the island's most sacred sites. Although it's not on our itinerary, this is what I propose we do: two hours' shopping here in the Old Quarter, followed by a short stroll to the fabled Mirror Wat."

Little Buddha beams, rubbing plump palms together.

"Remember," Mimi cautions, "to stay with the tour. We have brought along a small team of Tranquility Gummis as a security measure. Randarum is perfectly safe, of course, but you know from your own carefully guarded lives back home it's better to be secure than sorry."

Passengers stampede toward the open doors of the luxury-brand godowns. "Look, Heather," one woman calls to her friend, "Van Cleef & Arpels!" Small repeating firearms at the ready, the Gummis scurry after them.

AS BRIONY LEAVES THE Haider Ackermann godown, Mimi's flourishing her pennant once more. With their side-arm muzzles, the Gummis herd everyone toward the Mirror Wat, but piercing screams hinder their progress.

Safeties off, the Gummis encircle the passengers. The muscle-bound Gummi closest to Briony smells of cloves in the miasmic heat, like a great ham baking.

But it's only a local woman having some sort of seizure. She twists, turns, shouts at, and pummels the khaki-uniformed man attempting to restrain her. Breaking free, she throws herself to the cobblestones, where she rolls and froths, tearing out clumps of her hair. The man tries to calm her, but she kicks out so hard it's impossible for him to control her. He finally does succeed in dragging her toward a bench, where he sits on her. On she screeches, higher and higher. Her face gone crimson, tears wash down until her blouse turns transparent.

"What on earth happened? Why such an unholy racket? Won't someone give her a Xanax or something?" The passengers are all agog, discomfited by this inexplicable public outburst — too entranced to look away, too appalled to help.

Mimi sends a Gummi over to speak to the uniformed man even as the woman wails and thrashes beneath him.

The Gummi comes back to whisper in Mimi's ear. Her green pennant flaps tirelessly as everyone's prodded into an even tighter circle and slammed down a side street. Once a respectful distance has opened between the passengers and the distraught woman, Mimi deploys her bullhorn: "That poor, poor woman. She works as a cleaner at the Marni godown and often brings her little son, who's four, to help her — I gather he's good at stacking boxes and other tidying and light lifting. She keeps a sharp eye on him, and he knows he's not permitted to go out into the plaza. But today, with so many of us flooding the shops, he must have slipped away and that was that — in an instant he was gone."

Madame Rehbinder of the Swedish nitroglycerin Rehbinders raises her hand: "But surely this woman she is perhaps only overreacting? Children run off and lose their way, and it's only a matter of moments before they wander home again or are found by a kindly policeman, don't you think?"

"In many places this would be true, Madame Rehbinder." Mimi's pennant droops. "Not in Randarum.

The government's rigid one son/limitless daughters policy means boys are especially prized here and are regularly abducted by unscrupulous men in white vans. They're either whisked out of the country for resale on the mainland or taken to the interior to have their appearances altered and then auctioned off to well-to-do families desirous of a son to carry on the family name. Sometimes they're only blinded or otherwise maimed and set to work as beggars in neighbouring Santorum."

"Horrifying!" Mrs. Rehbinder's sky-blue eyes well up. "Surely we must do something for this poor woman."

"What can we do? This is not our country or our justice system. The police or the army—I gather they're indistinguishable here—have specific procedures for dealing with cases such as these."

"Isn't it possible that this woman will be reunited with her young son?"

"To be frank, Madame Rehbinder, it's highly unlikely. The kidnappers move so swiftly and are so skilled, it's rare that a boy, once taken, is ever recovered. This woman likely has other children, all daughters, at home. They will no doubt lessen the sting of her loss."

Madame Rehbinder persists. "Could we not give this poor woman a sum of money, not to ease her grief—for as the mother of four fine boys myself, all away and secure at good schools, I know this is sadly not possible—but to help her in her time of needs? I've no cash with me, of course"—the other passengers nod their unanimity in this—"however, once we are back on the ship I'm certain we can organize something special for her." She turns to the nearest Gummi: "Run back to Marni and get this woman's contact information."

Mimi glances at her watch. "We now have only a few minutes left to see the Mirror Wat. Because there is nothing further we can do at the moment to help this terrible situation, I propose we proceed there at once."

The Wat turns out to be just around the corner, a squat stucco building half-hidden by market stalls, souvenir-hawkers, snake-charmers, silk-twirlers, fakirs, touts, and teenage prostitutes of indeterminate sex. Street vendors rush up to the group to offer Christian LuBottom and Jiminy Chew stilettos, original tags still on.

Despite Mimi's best efforts, Briony notices dark mutterings rive the group. "How can we be expected," a man in a madras blazer wonders, "to enjoy anything after all we've just endured?"

Mimi butts her way through the pandemonium, knocking papaya-vendors and stoned sadhus out of her way.

Briony takes her place in the line leading to the narrow temple door. Before passing through the metal detector, an old blind woman in a Charlotte Church T-shirt gives her a searching pat-down. Temple guards prod her fellow passengers with billy clubs as they stumble along a dark corridor.

In bright red trousers not found anywhere off Martha's Vineyard, Mr. Harry Templeton of Templeton Templeton Dreggs arbitrageurs takes one guard's arm. "See here, young fellow, we have only now had the most harrowing experience. Please show some consideration."

The guard expectorates on Mr. Templeton's white

driving shoes while a colleague clubs his elbow. "Block no the doors," the guards all chant, "block no the doors."

They hurtle along through the dark. Maybelle Clabbers of the Boston Clabbers, who owned but did not sail on the *Mayflower*, goes down in a heap of summer-weight tweeds. Her unstranding pearls click across the paving, slip-sliding the rest of her cohort into an inner, dimensionless chamber.

In the sudden reflected light, Briony looks up in wonder. Mirrors cover every surface — walls, pillars, distant arches and trusses march toward infinity. Altars, reliquaries, trunked and crested deities glitter with silvered glass, shining everyone back at themselves faceted and dismembered. Briony watches as one of her eyes enfilades from column to column in the fathomless distance, while her lips, parted in astonishment, multiply horizontally, mixing and mingling with other passenger's facial features. Even the floor offers no relief, its brilliant surface warping everyone into funhouse delirium.

They all want to bolt, but how? When all is reflection, any movement accordions into space. Entry portal vanished and guards long gone, the blundering, panicky herd makes its way, un-nudes descending a plenitude of staircases.

"This is too much to bear," a scarlet mouth appears to enunciate into Briony's ear, though the sound emerges from somewhere far behind her. She turns to face it, but what mouth, which one? This one, that one — that stack of six over there? "It's hard," a woman torn to silky shards cries, "to grasp the strange beauty of this place when all

I can think of is that poor woman caterwauling in the street." "We came out for enjoyment and relaxation, to see the sights," a man sliced into every shade of taupe mutters, "and then to be so meanly interrupted. How will we ever find our way back to our prelapsarian selves?" A brindled moustache quivers in quintuplicate: "How she haunts me! Her cries pollute our pleasure."

A hieratic voice and flashes of coiled silver hair swarm round Briony. "How are we to unsee what we saw? How to unlearn her pain? She has turned our whole endeavour frivolous and foul."

"People!" The grandiose chamber echoes so powerfully Mimi needs no bullhorn. "Who will benefit from this self-castigation? Will pointing accusing fingers at ourselves lessen that woman's suffering in any way? We are on a cruise, and she lives on an island that has nothing to do with us. We visit her country and enjoy its generous exchange rate while Randarum profits from our expenditures. Who is harmed in this transaction? I suggest we return to our coaches now. In fifteen minutes, we'll be back aboard the *Emerald Tranquility* for preprandial drinks and dancing on Mikimoto Deck before First Seating!"

A portal opens in the mirroring and Mimi emerges, waving her pennant. Briony and the others follow, eager to be unreflective once more.

5

LUIS, ON HIS KNEES, applies the finishing touches to Briony's costume.

"Tell me the truth, Luis — am I too nude?"

"No such thing."

"Thank you."

He strews more kelp in her hair.

BY THE TIME SHE steps out onto Mikimoto Deck, it's already hopping in an osteoarthritic way.

She marvels once again at the limited imaginations of the rich, counting three Marie Antoinettes, one King Midas and his lamé-draped daughter or possibly niece, two Cleopatras, and a slouchy little guy in big glasses who's either a convincing Bill Gates or the ship accountant.

Mimi storms up, accompanied by a Barbarella complete with ray gun and black vinyl catsuit with transparent cutouts for her pert breasts.

"Gigot, you look fantastic," Briony says.

"You like? I have so much problems with my hair and the eyelashes."

"You are more beautiful than Jane herself."

Mimi looks Briony up and down. "What are you supposed to be?"

She points to her life preserver, which is fast deflating. "I am the drowned woman."

"This is why you are all painted blue," Gigot says. "You are chill from the sea." He kisses her azure cheeks. "Briony, you are always so *géniale*."

Mimi scowls. "I call it bad taste."

Briony takes in the older woman's long, plum-coloured gown. "What are you — a screaming pope?"

"So original," Gigot says.

"I am *not* in costume."

Gigot and Briony try for chastened looks.

Mimi turns to Briony. "You of all people should know better than to remind cruise passengers of drowning. Do you joke about plane crashes when you're flying first-class gratis?"

Briony tries to recall. "On Virgin, for sure."

"Do you mention guerrillas in the mountains when you write a destination piece on a popular Latin American capital? Or infant smog-deaths in a feature on Beijing dumplings?"

"Mimi, you're taking this far too seriously. It's a party — no one's leaping to eschatological conclusions."

Mimi looks at her quizzically. "What does that even mean?"

When a server glides up offering champagne, Briony slips away.

She resolves to spend the rest of the evening avoiding people she's met before and evading those she hasn't — her usual dance of social indifference. The only person she longs to see is nowhere to be found, so why's she even here? Once again, full-fathom five seems an increasingly attractive alternative to her chronic anomie.

Little Buddha rolls by, disguised as a gold-striped croquet ball sticked along by golden boys got up as mallets. Captain Kartoffeln, exhibiting a literary sensibility Briony hasn't suspected, pegs by as Ahab. A kicking line of white people in sombreros and leis congas past.

Heading for the desserts table she collides with a stately woman in a white columnar gown, her silver hair fixed in place by a clip of amethyst grapes.

"And who are you," Briony asks, "Athena, the goddess of wisdom?"

The old woman gives her a cool look. "I am Philautia, goddess of self-love. It makes all the other loves possible. Or impossible, I can never remember which."

"May I be your acolyte?"

"Sorry, my dear. I always travel light."

"Don't we all?"

The old woman laughs and glides away.

"Oh! Oh!" the revellers marvel as multicolour spotlights sweep Mikimoto Deck and fiery blooms explode across the night sky. "Ride of the Valkyries" slashes out of the sound system. Briony watches a big man in a bear suit pursue a young girl dressed as Anne of Green Gables. The girl's in tears as she dashes past. "Poor kid," Briony thinks, wondering if she should intervene.

She moves to block the bear when out of nowhere a troop of men appear on deck, all dressed in black — trainers, leggings, balaclavas, lifelike AK-47s with collapsible stocks. Almost dangerously realistic terrorists, Briony thinks. Mimi should see this if she wants bad taste.

She does see it—up close. One of the men has her by the scruff of her neck while another holds his weapon to her head. Briony hadn't suspected Mimi could be such a good sport. They must have rehearsed for hours. She looks genuinely panicked, tears pouring from her eyes.

Captain Kartoffeln holds his hands high in the air. Briony laughs: everyone's in on the act. Servers freeze in place, the conga line stops kicking.

A balaclava steps forward and speaks. Briony can't hear him over the booming fireworks and Wagnerian excess. Fireworks and something else.

Bullets! Briony realizes. They whizz by disturbingly close to her head. Verismo's one thing, she thinks, but this is overdoing it. She hits the deck.

So do the rest of the revellers who are able. Not easy to accomplish for those in Marie Antoinette *paniers* or with hip or knee replacements.

Balaclava guy shouts something. It sounds to Briony like "libation." They ought to give the poor guy a drink.

He begins again. "Universal Libation Farm!" An agrarian movement of some sort? At sea? She thinks this unlikely.

A smaller balaclava guy steps forward to translate, but with a pronounced speech impediment: "Univerthal Liberation Front demanth your attention!"

Slice. Clang. The little guy's head rolls across the deck as a blood-rimmed silver tray wobbles to a halt centimetres from Briony. The waiters are all Gummis in disguise.

Holding Mimi close, the original balaclava man shouts, "She dries! She dries!"

"Dies?" Captain Kartoffeln supplies.

"Purple lady dies, yes?"

"What do you want?"

"What?"

"What are your demands?"

"Dead capitalism."

"Death to capitalism?"

"Yes! All gold!"

"You want all our gold?"

"Yes!"

"Is this not a dialectical contradiction? Anti-capitalists wanting gold?"

"Sorry?"

"Will you take silver and platinum as well?"

"Sorry?"

Captain calls out: "Gummies, hold your fire. And your trays."

They reluctantly comply.

"And you," he shouts at the balaclava man, "release the purple lady and we will give you gold."

"Release?"

Like a demented game of telephone, Briony thinks, only more dire.

"Let her go!"

"Give gold, free lady!" He signals for his fellow bala-clavians to pass among the partygoers as they rip off necklaces and earrings and two tiaras, along with arm-fuls of wallets from the men.

They reassemble around a stricken Mimi.

"Let her go!" the captain commands.

Little Buddha, his boys knocking him along with no little skill, bowls fast into the hooded men, sending a number of them flying. Mimi makes a break for it. More trays slice the air. One, two, three balaclava heads, heavy as Halloween pumpkins, smash to the deck.

The captain pulls out his Luger and eliminates two more. Over the side scramble the remaining few. Briony hurries to the rail and watches as they rappel down the *Emerald Tranquility*'s scarped side and drop into a waiting Zodiac.

The Gummis take their places next to her, ready to shoot, but someone cries out, "Hold your fire! They've got another hostage." Jolting along in the Zodiac are the handful of surviving balaclavas, Barbarella at their centre.

"Gigot!" Briony calls out, but he's too tightly gagged to respond. The Zodiac zooms off. Glancing behind her, Briony sees Teenah has chosen this moment to make an appearance at last, done up in chartreuse silk and carrying between her beseeching legs a triangular green head. Following close behind is her mate and prey, an enormous decapitated mantis.

"Have we missed anything?" the headless creature asks.

BRIONY KNOCKS. Eventually the door to Mimi's suite swings open. She stands, peaked in the boat-wash morning light, bereft of make-up and sporting a golden sequin skullcap. She pulls a startled Briony into a fervent embrace.

"Mimi — are you okay?"

Without answering, she drags Briony into her still-darkened suite with its unexpected mortuary smells and dials up the light.

"People have been so kind." Extravagant flower arrangements, mountainous fruit and cheese baskets, jeroboams of champagne crowd every surface.

Tears flood Mimi's wincing eyes. "How can I ever thank them enough?" She locks Briony in her arms once more. "But only you — *you!* — thought to come in person."

It was the cheapest solution she could come up with. Does Mimi have any idea how much a consoling spray of cymbidiums costs at Tender Tendrils Florists down on Fabergé Deck?

"She has not this entire night long into slumber slipped." Little Buddha emerges from Mimi's bedroom. She grasps his hands. "Praun has been such a deep help to me, I cannot begin to tell you."

"The sedatives the ship doctor gave our Mimi did nothing to speed her into the arms of Morpheus."

"When I close my eyes, I see those poor boys and hear the awful sound of their heads hitting Mikimoto Deck."

"Perhaps a short meditation followed by the chanting of a Mahayana sutra or two in order to soothe the turbulent soul?" He touches the tip of her nose. She giggles.

"Oh, Praun."

"Would you care to join us, sweet Briony?"

"I don't want to intrude."

Mimi hugs her once more. "But you're family, Briony."

"I truly wish I could" — she gently detaches herself from Mimi's clutch — "but I have a big deadline — 500 words about the *Emerald Tranquility* for *Euphoria!*"

The old PR Mimi clicks back into action. "Did I tell you, Praun, our Briony is a travel journalist?"

He studies Briony with new interest. "Like poor little Fagot?"

"Gigot, darling. GHEE-goh." Mimi makes to hug her once more, but Briony steps back in time. "Poor fellow."

"I'm sure he'll be fine," Briony offers.

"Are you?"

Not at all. "Of course — Gigot's a survivor."

"Most perceptive, our fair Briony. We will chant for him. But perhaps you and I should meet at some later time. I have the most superlative idea for a travel article I wish to share with you."

He and every day tripper Briony's ever met. He has an idea; all she has to do is write it up.

"I even have a title." Of course he does. "'All Desire Is Suffering: You, Moksha, and the Luxury Cruise.'"

Briony smiles her thanks for this invaluable inspiration while her hand scrambles behind her for the doorknob.

Mimi's left eyelid has sunk to half-mast. "There's a new angle for you."

"Isn't it?" Briony feels slightly bilious.

"We want, we need, we desire so many things." Mimi's open eye emits a spectral glow. "And then SLICE!"

—— she slashes an index finger across her own throat——
"Decapitation! Plop, plop, plop."

Little Buddha pulls her to him. "Come, my dear.
Together we will contemplate the vanity of human
wishes." He leads her toward the bedroom door. Briony
slips out.

6

"WE ARE CRUISING AT 20 KNOTS, or 37.04 kilometres per hour, which in miles would come to —" Captain Kartoffeln stands before the bridge's wide windshield curve. Banks of monitors blip and blink behind him. The monotonous grey sea stretches out to the monstrous grey sky. A dozen trim young men in whites surround the captain, echoing his blanched presence. What a font of tedious nautical stats he is, Briony reflects. The numerous decks and their glittering names, the elevators and escalators and all their locations, ditto for lifeboats and life jackets (in your entry-hall closet). Teenah promised to be here but isn't. Briony tries not to picture her in bed with the insect.

"Petrossian, Limoges, and Hermès Decks all offer refined staterooms with spacious balconies, while Birkin and Waterford Rooms feature large picture windows. Halston, Hummel, Anthracite, and Zircon Decks feature cabins that are masterpieces of compact design and water-tightness." Electronic doors wheeze open. Briony wonders at the way Teenah's dressed for 14:13 — her sundress a flash of pale gossamer.

As feared, she comes attached: the mantis, all in black couture today, from his distressed leather jacket to his drop-crotch jodhpurs and patent-leather biker boots.

She has seen Teenah with other men before, other

women too. Why shouldn't she be with anyone she fucking well pleases, Briony considers, attempting to regain her equanimity. But she had imagined many more moments of noncommittal nautical bliss with Teenah. How likely will this be with this desiccated creature along for the ride?

Teenah glides over to breathe on her cheeks. "Have you met Kurd?" she asks Briony.

"Not really."

"Directly below us, on Lanvin Deck," the captain drones on, "you will find the splendid Palm Court for elegant soirées."

"Briony, please meet my friend Kurd Fenstermacher—I'm sure you've heard of him."

She has—only one of the world's most famous starchitects—but why should she admit that? He reaches out an arm ending in spindly fingers—it's like shaking hands with a rake.

"Ah," he exclaims, "Teenah's enticing American friend."

"Canadian," Teenah whispers in his drooping El Greco ear.

"*Bitte?*"

"Briony's Canadian."

"No wonder she is so fresh, so apple-fed and beguilingly frosty." His tensile arm lengthens round Briony's waist. Teenah peels the creeping appendage away. "Kurd takes a little getting used to."

"Do I not?"

Briony finds his grin a macro-aggression, his big blinding teeth insufferable. His physical presence creates a force field enclosing Teenah and her in his attenuated domain. "I will grow on you, I assure you."

The captain breaks off listing the ship's entertainment venues to give them a nasty look. "If I am to relay this important ship information to you, I must respectfully ask you to please pay close attention."

"I've heard," Teenah says, "there's a below-deck discothèque called Truffle Butter?"

The captain lowers his head for some serious beard stroking. "Will you tell me, please, where you've heard this absurd name?"

"If I rat them out will you make them walk the plank?" The rumbling noise low in the captain's throat doesn't quite constitute laughter.

"Your informants, please."

"Just some girls at the gym."

His brow darkens. "These girls, they work in the gym?"

Teenah prevaricates. "They were working out at the gym. I didn't get their names."

"But can you confirm" — Kurd jumps in, one countryman appealing to another — "there is a lower-deck discothèque?"

"I cannot confirm or deny, but if there were such a below-deck venue, it would of course be off-limits to passengers."

"How come?" A young girl Briony hasn't noticed before fiddles with an astrolabe-like instrument, lime Popsicle bobbing in and out of her pursed mouth. Gold coins have been woven into her strawberry blond hair. Anne of Green Gables from the costume party!

"Cecily" — Mimi lowers her voice as if speaking to a total dolt — " the *Emerald Tranquility* has a strict non-fraternization policy."

The girl gives her Popsicle an angry lick. "I don't even know what that means."

"Passengers aren't allowed to consort with the crew."

"'Consort'?"

"Hang out with," Teenah offers.

"We find," Mimi says, "it's more conducive to creating a harmonious shipboard ambience."

"Why can't you just speak English?" Popsicle dripping green onto her pink romper, she runs from the room, the drama of her exit impeded by the sluggish automatic doors.

"Who was *that*?" Teenah asks.

"Everyone knows little Cecily," Mimi says. "She's Margot Tybor's granddaughter."

"Margot Tybor?" The captain swoons. "She's on my ship? Why was I not informed?"

"I thought she was dead," Kurd says.

"She is dead," Mimi says. She turns to the captain: "Calm down, Wülf."

"Who's that?" Teenah asks.

"Only the greatest eastern European star of the post-war era," the captain says.

"She worked with everyone," Kurd adds. "Antonioni, Bergman, Visconti, Peckinpah. Who can forget her wonderful turn in Fassbinder's *The Scalding Despair of Rota Gravure*?"

Captain Kartoffeln breaks in. "And when her great beauty began to dim, Margot revitalized her career by starring in West Germany's longest-running and most hilarious sitcom, *Willst Du Ins Kino Gehen?*"

"How this show makes me laugh, even now in the reruns," Kurd says. "Ah, when she puts the cheese up the little dog's—"

"And places the baby on the BMW's roof and her groceries in the small *Kindersitz!*" the captain laughs so heartily tears trickle down his hirsute cheeks. "Perhaps you should go see if little Cecily's all right," he says to Mimi. "She seems such a sensitive child."

Mimi looks startled. "Child? She's thirty-two, Wülf."

It's the captain's turn to look surprised, "We will follow you, Mimi, and go to the elevators, yes?"

THEIR LITTLE GROUP CRAMS into a glass-sided capsule that drops them down through the decks as though they are plummeting into an ant farm. "Okay, check this out," Teenah murmurs to Briony and Kurd. "You will notice a certain darkening."

"How so?" Kurd says.

"At bridge level everyone's white—passengers and crew—except me, of course. The crew are all even dressed in white."

As the elevator whisks them past the stateroom, entertainment, and dining decks, Teenah points out crew members with pale brown skin in beige uniforms. "Down a few levels, the maids are mainly South Asian, the butlers South American or Middle Eastern." The elevator slips below decks: in their grey uniforms, the cleaners, laundry-room workers, and maintenance people fall on a skin-tone gradient between mahogany and ebony.

"Wow," Kurd says. "With the many cruise ships I have been on, why have I never noticed this?"

Teenah sticks out her tiny tongue. "You don't need to, my pasty-white friend."

The elevator lets them out on Zero Deck, where they troop through a succession of white-painted chambers linked by watertight doors that beep, whistle, and grind as they open at their approach and close with a metallic thud.

They stop in the largest, most deafening chamber, where a half-dozen diesel engines throb. As the captain bellows out his spiel, Kurd cranes his neck, entranced by every lever, pipe, gear, dial, gauge, bolt, and vat in his path.

Exiting the pulsing room, Briony feels her skull has been hollowed out with a stave. Her ears seem more spacious now too, chirring with a high insect whine.

They pass through the Fresh-Water Production Room, with its snaking white pipes, monumental green-painted tanks, and swimming pool–chlorine smell, and the Fuel Treatment Chamber, which stinks of diesel and an absent crew member's curried lunch.

They reach what Briony takes to be a gigantic laundry room. Big stainless steel machines with frontal portholes churn and froth. How strange, she thinks — the ship washes laundry with yellow detergent. Except no garments swirl inside the big rotating drums. An acrid smell catches up with her: these white machines spin small oceans of heaving urine.

"People often wonder," the captain says, "what a great ship does with its waste, liquid or solid." What Briony wonders is if they're laundering the pee to make the water potable once more.

Over the roar of the machines, Kurd asks pertinent questions about three-mile limits and whether the *Emerald Tranquility* doesn't, like most other hulking cruise liners, simply dump its shit over the side.

The captain goes quite red, sputters boilerplate regarding floating hygiene, purification, and evacuation — unfortunate diction, Briony feels — sustainability, biodiversity, and renewing the integrity of the oceans. Confirmation, in other words, they do dump it over the side to the tune of 50,000 litres a day.

Rather than contemplate excretory volume further, Teenah and Briony duck down a red-lit passageway.

"This is insane," Teenah says. "When they said ship tour I thought they meant an hour or something. This is Teutonically thorough. Kurd's in his element, though. Architects! Takes him four hours to buy a screw at the hardware store."

"If the ship's so fucking green," Briony asks, "why do I get fresh, full-size shampoo, facial moisturizer, body moisturizer, masking gel, night-regenerating oil, and I forget what else every single day, even if I've only used a drop or two?"

Teenah looks thoughtful.

"What's wrong?" Briony asks.

"You hate him, don't you?"

"'Hate' is such a strong word.'"

"Loathe?"

Briony shakes her head.

"Abhor? Execrate?"

"Please."

"Dread?"

"Warmer."

"Oh Briony, I felt all these things the first time I met him. He's so off-putting and yet somehow compelling. Negative charisma, I think it's called. I have rather sprung him on you, but I couldn't think how else to tell you in a way that wouldn't—"

"Trigger suicidal ideation? Teenah, you've formed a couple with him!"

"Where is this jealousy coming from? The whole idea of coupledom usually gives you the bends. Anyhow, we're not a couple."

"You aren't?"

"We're fellow travellers. We enjoy each other's company. It's a lot like when you and I hang out, except he's capable of staying around longer than an hour or two."

Briony's determined not to be the besotted person who says, "But you said—" She can't help herself: "But you said—"

"Watch out, Briony!"

She crashes into an old guy in a lab coat carrying a tray clinking with test tubes full of a sludgy substance unidentifiable until a dozen of them crash to the floor and— voila!—instant recognition. The stocky young woman following close behind plows into the old guy too, and the remaining test tubes shatter.

"Holy shit!" Briony cries out redundantly.

"Oh, most beautiful ladies, I'm so sorry." The old man and the young woman shoo them back along the corridor. "Fecal sample testing, you see. It must be done many times each day to determine pH levels and the like."

He opens a narrow red door almost concealed behind intersecting pipes. "Please come in while I ring for the cleaners."

Picking up a handset, he motions them to sit on a narrow bed covered with a scarlet and blue spread emblazoned with a big yellow star. The young woman crowds in with them, smelling of baby powder and corrosive disinfectant. When he finishes his call the old man takes the mini-armchair, opens the middle drawer of his built-in desk, and removes four cognac miniatures — Hine Rare vsop.

"This is your office?" Teenah studies the black and white photos covering one wall.

"Office!" the young woman snorts derisively.

"Office *and* quarters." He pours the amber liquid out into clean test tubes.

"You don't even have a window," Briony says.

The young woman rolls her eyes. "Windows for passengers only, you silly girl."

The old man turns on a monitor set into one wall. A 3-D tropical rainforest comes up: a simulated darting drone view of rare butterflies, lavish birds, and other already-extinguished species as they flit about the verdant digital canopy. "There are seventeen different channels, from 'Southern Pampas RV Tour' to 'Tokyo Fish Market

Slosh' to 'Wild-Horse Gallop across the Steppe.' I lack for nothing."

Briony tries to conceal her dismay at his constricted life, his straitened room. His bright protuberant eyes miss nothing.

"You needn't pity me." He indicates a narrow-gauge door she hadn't noticed. "I even have my own jakes."

"His own what?" Teenah whispers to Briony.

"Toilet."

"Open it," he says.

Briony can reach the handle without rising from the bed. Inside is a machine-tooled chamber for washing, urinating, defecating, and showering.

"Your maids, your butlers, your common cleaners — many have only a toilet and sink in their room with a shower down the hall. Most share a cabin of this size. Maids and cleaners are four to a cabin. You begin to understand how deluxe my digs are? At least I have a home, which is more than many can say in these desperate times."

Shit, Briony thinks, embarrassed as a tear trickles down her cheek.

"Aie!" the young woman cries. "Six in mine, no jakes."

The old man places a wizened hand on Briony's shoulder. "I'm sorry. I didn't mean to sadden you. My name is Viktor, by the way. Viktor with a 'k.'"

Wiping away her tear, she shakes his hand. "I'm Briony. No need to apologize, Viktor. Something in my eye."

"And this is Anna May — Anna May Wang."

"A pleasure," Teenah says, shaking her hand. "How long have you been on the *Emerald Tranquility*?"

"Five years," Anna May says. "Five years too long."

"Fourteen for me," Viktor adds. "Before that another twenty years on several different ships of varying quality."

"Where are you from originally?"

"None of your business," Anna May says.

Viktor places his hand over his heart. "I'm from here."

Teenah laughs. "No, where are you really from?"

"I really am from here."

Briony persists. "But where were you born?"

"Where I was born is no longer there. Where I grew up, the same. The family, the village, the nation — all gone. It's easier just to say I'm from here, saving both time and face for all."

They all knock back their drinks. Viktor produces more miniatures from his drawer, which appears to replenish itself as miraculously as the chocolate truffle box on Briony's mantelpiece.

"Muzeeka!" He holds out the remote. Flutes, drums, bells, a woman's high nasal voice backed by a children's choir flood the cabin. It's unclear to Briony whether they sing in an actual language or are simply scatting about. Anna May's broad hands clap along.

"Oh," Teenah says, "I know where you are from."

Viktor squirms in his chair. "Where?"

"Here. You, Viktor, are definitely from here. You've found your home."

"But how solemn we've become on this pleasure cruise for luxury people. Drink up, my beautiful ladies, for there is always more. On the great ship *Emerald Tranquility*, there's always more than more."

Briony studies a small black and white photo above his desk. "Is this your father, Viktor?"

"No, that's my uncle. My Uncle Ho." He smiles with downcast eyes.

Anna May makes a meaty fist and thrusts it in the air.

"TEE — AAA — N-G-O, TEE — AAA — N-G-O,"
Mrs. Nightingale "Nighty" Sweeney barks the steps in
Briony's ear as she barges her across the dance floor at
the Begin the Beguine Nightclub on Schiaparelli Deck.
Briony's locked in Nighty's fierce embrace at the *Emerald
Tranquility*'s 15:00 dance class, "Tango with Brad and
Kiki," because Teenah's otherwise occupied. Brad and
Kiki are twins and, as they never tire of reminding the
class, prize-winning professional ballroom dancers with
their own Antipodean chain of studios back in Australia.

Here they shark about the sprung birch floor, staring into each other's eyes with an avidity that discomfits
Briony. Brad's never available to dance with surplus
women, of which there are many, but Kiki will occasionally venture forth with one of the men, sure-footed old
duffers in navy blazers and clouds of Creed Vetiver.

"Who are your people, dear?" Nighty coos in the
way of rich women everywhere trying to ferret out one's
net worth. As a Canadian, Briony feels she has a certain advantage in composing a burnished life narrative,
since rich Americans — any Americans, really — know
nothing of her home and native land. They nevertheless
pretend to recognize the lustre of the names she drops:
Miss Edgar's and Miss Cramp's, Havergal, Lower Canada

College, Upper Canada College, the Bridle Path and, in moments of sheer desperation, McGill.

"My late mother," she begins, "was a McConnell, my father a Thomson and a bit of a bohemian: he painted. They perished in an unfortunate gondola mishap on the Grand Canal during *Carnevale*. I was quite young."

Nighty shakes her jowls sadly.

"People!" Either Brad or Kiki's amped falsetto cuts the air. "We're going to pick up the pace a bit, so lift those shoulders, elongate your spines, and tighten those buns."

"How old were you, Briony?"

"Um, nine." Briony's endlessly inventive but tends to fall down on specifics. "My grandmother — my mother's mother — took me in."

"TEE — AAA — N-G-O, TEE — AAA — N-G-O," Nighty huffs as she flings Briony into a *cangrejo*. "And your grandmother resided where?"

Briony chuckles reminiscently. "She had this big old mock-Tudor barn of a place on Georgian Bay."

Nighty lunges without warning.

"It all became too much," Briony continues. "Finding and keeping proper staff began to weigh on her. When I went away to uni she was finally forced to sell. It broke her heart to see the old place converted into fourteen luxury condos."

"I can only imagine." Nighty mists up. "When I lost Brock I had to let Candlewood go. It's a country club now, don't you know. Popular with a crowd I don't frequent." She spasms slightly.

These old WASP dames, Briony thinks, it's only a matter

of time before genteel anti-Semitism surfaces. She doesn't know who she despises more, Nighty for her bigotry, or herself for having served up this kowtowing performance.

A large, spotted hand comes down on Nighty's shoulder. She and Briony look up at a tawny face and topaz eyes looming above them.

"May I cut in?"

She hips Nighty aside and draws Briony to her. Does this majestic woman never end? Briony marvels.

"I am Mrs. Moore. Who might you be?"

Briony tells the old woman her name, wondering at the heat she gives off. She notices the amethyst grapes in her twining silver hair. "You're Philautia, goddess of narcissism or something."

Mrs. Moore tilts her head skeptically. "Am I?"

"That's what you said at the costume party."

"I say a lot of things. Shall we get on with this?"

Her chin against Briony's forehead, Mrs. Moore moves without reciting mnemonic letters. Stride, stride, dip dip dip, turn. One silver sandal slides down Briony's bare calf while strong fingers sleek her spine. Briony's feet fail her during *la corrida*, but Mrs. Moore canters them through. At some point Briony realizes she has no responsibility here and lets go of all agency.

She's vaguely aware even Brad and Kiki have stopped to stare along with the others. Now Briony's hyperventilating.

Brad clicks off the music. Mrs. Moore and Briony freeze, entangled. "That's all, people!" — Kiki says with a beacon smile — "See you Thursday. Good class!"

Briony and Mrs. Moore stand apart. "You're pretty good at this," the old woman says. "It's so rare to find another passenger who knows anything at all." She walks away.

NEW DAWN. NEW BEGINNING.

New life.

Briony awakes feeling all these things.

She rises to meet the day.

Where Mrs. Moore is not: Walk on Water Promenade with its weighted vests and messianic overtones. Leviathan Lending Library. Nautilus Needlepoint Nook. Lukewarm Yoga in the Doris Mindlessness Studio. Make Better Vacay iPad Videos in the DigitalServices@Sea Genius Room. Pelagic Pilates with Pam beside the newly enlarged Poseidon Pool. Seafarers' Smorgasbord in the Triton Bistro, where vibrant world cuisines get beaten into bland submission ("Ask about Our Pre-Chewed Options!"). Mrs. Moore has vanished.

Briony races down the atrium spiral stair to Reception, fabricating a likely ploy on the fly. Mrs. Moore has left behind her antique silver pill case, cashmere cardigan, emerald bracelet, one opal earring, Ativan, earbuds, remote for her pacemaker, glucose monitor.

Ms. Pert at Reception proves hard to get by: "Unfortunately, we're not allowed to give out stateroom numbers. If you'd care to leave the item with us, we'll ring your friend with the good news."

Oh, snap! Briony only now remembers she has left the

item in question in her suite. Perhaps Ms. Pert could ring Mrs. Moore so Briony might speak with her. Ms. Pert's eyes slide sideways as she listens to the phone ringing in her headset. "I'm so sorry, but Mrs. Moore doesn't seem to be responding."

Dashing off, Briony scans the audience for "Whither the Middle East?" at the Global Issues Kaffeeklatsch, with special guest speaker from the Israeli Ministry of Homeland Security and Apartheid. She checks out the green-tinted hoofers at the "Salute to *Wicked* Revue" in the Broadway Melody Theatre. Oldsters slump before looped reruns of Johnny Carson's *Tonight Show* in the Boob-Tube Room. "Rex Reed — Live! — Recalls the Stars!" in Hideaway Hut turns out to be empty save for the man himself, dozing in one corner.

Briony turns to face the glass curtain wall of the Full-Fathom Five Tearoom, where the Guo Hua Chinese Brush Painting class is already in progress. Amid the white-haired heads bowed in concentration over their brushes, lucid sea-light radiates from the cluster of amethyst grapes in Mrs. Moore's hair.

The old, insouciant Briony would have barged right in — "Sorry I'm late, Tai Chi with Teri ran over" — but her fresh new incarnation, circumspect, mindful, holds back.

The universe delivers. The teacher begins gathering up brushes and spilling out bowls of grey water into the sink. Mrs. Moore holds her drawing up to the light — bamboo shoots delicately rendered — then turns it so an ancient woman in an embroidered silk tunic can see. Mrs. Moore says something and tears the drawing in two, bins it. She and the ancient woman laugh and, murmuring together, walk toward the exit.

Should she feign surprise at running into Mrs. Moore here? Or abandon all reticence and run to greet her with effusive cries? Far better, she considers, to hold back, show some restraint — wait for Mrs. Moore to notice her rather than bounding up like a needy puppy.

Time has slowed, soft light gone wavery. Mrs. Moore glances her way and then away, eyes devoid of recognition. She doesn't see Briony at all! Mrs. Moore places her hand on the ancient woman's arm and steers her toward the elevators.

Briony flies after her. "Mrs. —! Mrs. —!" In her panic she has forgotten her name. "Mrs. Moore!"

The older women enter the elevator, and the doors begin to slide together. In the last sliver of space, Mrs. Moore notices Briony, appears to register who she is — the doors thump closed. Illuminated numerals mark her ascent.

Briony makes for the stairs and catches up to the elevator at its final destination as the doors open on Wraith Deck. The sea spangles on all sides but the mirrored cage is empty save for Briony's own fractalled face.

"Briony! *Briony*!"

Teenah waves from a distant sunbed. Disturbingly slender, Kurd elongates next to her in black crochet trunks, a Giacometti on holiday. Yesterday Teenah was everything. Now she's with Kurd. Briony finds herself swiftly re-evaluating their "relationship." Can she truly want a woman, luscious though she is, who wants creepy Kurd?

All around lie old people in various states of undress, many of them already medium-well.

"Do sit down, Briony." Kurd taps the sunbed next to his. "You're making me unrelaxed." He holds out a silver flask. Briony leans away. "You mustn't be afraid of me, you know. I don't bite, or when I do, leave no scars other than emotional ones."

He proffers the flask once more.

Briony sniffs the spout, expecting something strong and alcoholic, not the earthy sweetness of a rice paddy after heavy rain.

"*Papaver somniferum,*" Kurd explains. "Opium tea. Good for *mal de mer* and what have you."

"I've had opium tea before — it never smelled like this," she says.

"That's the ambergris I mix in."

"Ambergris?"

"A bile-duct secretion found in the intestines of sperm whales. Raw, it has a more excremental odor that sweetens with age. Please try."

She takes a sip. Two — it goes down a treat. She offers the flask to Teenah, who waves it away. "Kurd drinks that shit all day long. Makes me costive."

"Please tell me, my dear Briony," Kurd says, "what do you think of this cruise, apart from the terrible farrago of the costume party?"

"It feels like every cruise I've ever taken, only even more claustrophobic and superannuated."

"Any news of poor Gigot?" Teenah asks as she rubs sunblock on her thighs. "Poor fellow."

With a start, Briony realizes she has forgotten the party, forgotten poor Gigot. "I didn't know you knew him."

"Doesn't everyone know Gigot? Such a darling."

"That perky little bum of his," Kurd adds.

"I hope he'll be all right."

"I worry about what will happen when they discover he isn't Barbarella," Briony says.

Kurd takes another swig. "They were Muslim pirates, no?"

Teenah looks offended. "Why do you think that? Because they had dark skin and black eyes?"

"And big black beards," Kurd says. "I watched when the Gummis removed the balaclavas of those who lost their heads. The captain thought they might be from Indonesia."

"So they'll chop Gigot's head off when they discover he isn't the young Jane Fonda?" Teenah's eyes overflow.

"Don't be so sure. Islamist countries may profess to hate queers, but in my experience the men are among the most homosocial in the world—that may count for something." He turns to Briony. "He is tough, our Gigot?"

Briony considers. "Not the first word that comes to mind."

"I keep imagining the worst," Teenah sobs. "What if—"

The poolside tranquility's shattered by an *a cappella* rendition of "Tainted Love."

"What the fuck is that?" Briony asks.

Wiping away her tears with a towel, Teenah nods toward the Wide Sargasso Sea whirlpool, which is full of blond young men. "It's just the Whiffs."

"The what?"

"Whiffenpoofs. From Yale."

Briony grimaces. "What's an Ivy League boys choir doing on the *Emerald Tranquility*?"

"I am surprised you haven't seen them before," Kurd says. "They are all about, singing Cole Porter medleys and 'The Lion Sleeps Tonight.' The oldies love them."

"They're giving me such a pain," Briony says.

"But Briony, they're all so sweet," Teenah protests.

"Bunch of rich kids on a rich boat full of rich geezers. Nothing sweet about it."

"Yes," Kurd says. "This is so often the case when too many rich people gather in one location. This I can never become accustomed to. But are you not yourself rich, dear Briony?"

She shakes her head.

"No? You are most convincing."

"Thank you," Briony says. "Protective colouration." The Whiffenpoofs have segued into "Lush Life." "They're ruining my favourite song."

Teenah turns to Kurd. "Briony works as a luxury-travel journalist. We first met years ago at a squalid club in Berlin where she was pretending to be rich and I was pretending to be poor. She was so convincing even then. Now I no longer need to pretend. I am poor."

Briony reaches for the flask again. "Since when?"

Teenah tosses her head. "Just because my mother's rich,

because my family is rich back to ten generations, doesn't automatically mean I am rich myself."

"Teenah summarily rejects the transitive power of wealth" — Kurd gulps down the last of the tea and tosses the flask into his Shigeru Gang Bang tote — "ever since she studied with Monsieur Piketty at EHESS."

Briony's eyes widen. "Come again?"

Teenah laughs. "My thesis adviser at *l'École des hautes études en sciences sociales.* 'Inheritance is capitalism at its worst. Wealth originating in the past automatically grows more rapidly, even without labour, than wealth stemming from work, which can be saved.' Anyway, it's not as though you live in want, Kurd. How else could you afford this cruise?"

"She's right," Kurd says to Briony. "I have much money, very much more than I need, but perhaps not more than I can spend in one lifetime. Yet I do not consider myself rich."

"No?"

The Whiffenpoofs clamber out of the whirlpool, still in full voice.

"I work for the rich, as I must if I am to live my best life and be the best architect I can be, but I can't say their ubiquity or their patronage endears them to me. Rather to the contrary: they make me always aware of the difference between my money and their wealth — the difference between this swimming pool and that ocean. You must feel this as well, Briony, as a journalist writing for a magazine appealing to the rich. What is it called?"

"*Euphoria!*"

The Whiffenpoofters chase one another among the sunbeds, flicking large white towels.

"But I know this magazine—it has the most ravishing fonts! As a writer for *Euphoria!* you are like this little remora clinging to the underbelly of the great capitalist behemoth. You look, dress, and comport yourself as if rich, yet as a luxury journalist you are merely a suckerfish feeding on the great and magnanimous host's feces. You and I, my dear, are fish of a feather."

Briony notices the Whiffenpoofs have caught one of the pool boys and are tossing him high in the air. Toss. Toss.

"You put things so well, Kurd," Briony says. "Neither of us born to wealth—if we stop sucking, we die. But even if Teenah rejects the obscene wealth of her family, it will still crash down on her one day like a tsunami. This is inevitable."

Teenah stares into Briony's eyes. "No, it's not."

"Teenah has been disinherited," Kurd says.

"No!" In an instant Briony comprehends why Kurd's an absolute necessity for Teenah. The androgyne she'd always thought of as a beautiful renegade turns out to need a patron. No, not a patron, for Teenah produces nothing. A sponsor.

Lying back in her sunbed so her glossy hair spreads out like a dark halo, Teenah sighs. "You remember when Mother called me back home to consult on that five-star she wanted to build on the river next to the Mint? I agreed at the time, thinking, how long can one hotel take? But by the time I arrived on site, the five-star had turned into a seven-star, seventeen discreet villas had become

370 extravagant ones, and one hotel had blossomed into a pan-Asian chain of twenty-seven, all thanks to Mother's inability to think small.

"That's when she introduced me to the architect for the newly christened Azure Heavens Above mega-project. I liked Kurd immediately — well, eventually — even as I realized I could end up tangled up in Asia for years to come. My idea of perfect horror. So I told her no, something no true Asian child should ever say to a true Asian parent. I would no longer project manage. And that was that. I am no longer her heir, no longer her son, or even her daughter for that matter. That suits me fine."

Briony is dubious about how long Teenah's filial rebellion will last. Good thing she's got her new leviathan to suck on. As Kurd spreads sun lotion across his concave belly, a phrase pops up in her mind, bright as a billboard: "I am not so afraid of the dark night as the friends I do not know." Must be poetry, she thinks, though she hasn't read much since leaving uni. It always promised so much while delivering so little.

"What a trio of coprophagists we are," Kurd says.

"Not so different," Briony adds, "from all those little people out there in the dark who suck it up all their lives."

The Whiffenpoofs, midway through "I Enjoy Being a Girl," throw the pool boy higher still. His good-natured laughter has taken on a frantic edge.

8

FOR WANT OF A better plan, Briony signs up for the Silk Route Showroom/Mysteries of the Tea Ceremony shore excursion, figuring this could be just the thing a Mrs. Moore sort of person might fancy.

Debarking late — Luis had uncharacteristically forgotten to steam her culottes — she finds there's only one remaining coach, already commandeered by Mimi and Little Buddha.

"Briony!" Mimi envelops her in her saffron gauze wrappings. When she gives a desultory wave of her seahorse pennant, a whiff of stale incense funk wafts off her. Is that a love bruise Briony spies on Little Buddha's neck?

She takes in the half-empty coach. "Where is everyone, Mimi?"

"The first coach was packed," she says loudly, then whispers, "It left not even half-full. I don't understand why; we've been promoting the hell out of it — 20% off for over-90s. It's always been one of our most popular excursions. Who doesn't love silk and tea?"

"Fear of death!" Little Buddha blurts out.

Mimi tries to shush him as the coach rumbles forth.

"You may not simply erase one missing passenger."

"Darling, a missing *journalist*." She pats Briony's hand. "Forgive my frankness, but you know what I mean."

"Regardless of his position," Little Buddha says, "Gigot's spectre must haunt every mind."

"We don't know Gigot's dead," Briony points out.

"You are most optimistic," he says. "When something like this happens on a ship, every person will be thinking, 'How safe am I on either ship or shore?'"

Mimi caresses his bare shoulder, which quivers like aspic at her touch. "You don't know passenger mentality, Little B. These people got where they are by ignoring the worst. Whatever the disaster, they will go on, impervious."

"'Impervious'?"

"Oblivious. The worst has happened. The pirate attack was efficiently quelled, no one killed but the pirates themselves. One non-passenger MIA. Pretty modest casualty list, no?"

Little Buddha's face darkens. "But Mimi, where is your compassion?"

"I know this sounds cold. Our passengers aren't mean-spirited or callous, only wonderfully skilled at self-protection."

Bizarre, Briony thinks, it's raining inside the coach. Is the sunroof open? And her eyes burn — allergy? pollution?

"But Briony," Little Buddha points out, "you weep."

She feels "weep" overstates the case. Two small tears only. "I miss Gigot."

Little Buddha's cephalopodan arms encircle her. *He is love*, she thinks, even as his hands graze her nipples. She's horrified at how maudlin she's become.

"Should we tell her?" Mimi whispers to Little Buddha.

"Tell me what?"

"The captain told us a frosted wig was found washed up on a beach in Kota Kinabalu. He said it's amazing how well the back-combing held."

"Oh no!" Briony wails.

"Group hug!" Mimi cries.

They stand together in Little Buddha's consoling, questing arms.

Briony feels safe, warm, vaguely nauseated.

THE GLASSY SPIRES OF *El Supuesto Palacio de Patos Blancos de Cultura y Comercio* dazzle. At second glance Briony sees their sheeny transparency reveals floor after floor seemingly devoid of people, furniture, culture, or merchandise.

Only the wide fountains footing the spires appear lively, aswim with multitudes of quacking white ducks that, according to Mimi, are sacred to the deeply spiritual Modigli people. The fowls' viscous droppings slick the white marble plaza, destabilizing more than a few of the *Emerald Tranquility*'s less nimble passengers. Poor Doña Cuantos Cuantos-Besos of the Buenos Aires bauxite dynasty might have slid clean off but for the reflexes of the Gummi who caught hold of her mantilla.

The passengers pour out of the elevators on the four-teenth storey of the *palacio*, a grand showroom of curving glass and crystal chandeliers dimly reflected in the marble floor.

Disentangling herself from Little Buddha, Mimi steps forth to greet the silk guide, a slender young woman in a silk *chamsong* embroidered over with tiny white ducks. When the woman begins to speak, it's clear her English is adequate, but her hands communicate even more eloquently as they form first a mulberry bush, followed by the silkworm itself, and a bent crone working a handloom.

Just as the woman's deft fingers create the unfurling of a floating shimmer of silk, Mimi whacks her delicately with her pennant.

"I'm sorry to interrupt your most interesting and lengthy performance, my dear, but we're on a tight itinerary. As you can see, the attention of many of our group has already wandered."

Most of the passengers have gathered before a wide stretch of glass where they contemplate a nearby building, roughly the same height as the *palacio,* a much older structure of water-stained concrete, rusted rebar sprouting from blasted walls, and sagging ceilings.

Briony notices its great windows have been opened in the midday heat, revealing hundreds of workers — men and women of all ages, along with adolescents and small children, all dressed in white. The men wear only dhotis, the women cumbersome saris, the children loincloths or tattered camisoles.

"Here you see the whole process before you." The guide gestures toward the decrepit building. "Please note the mulberry bushes down in the lobby. Worms eat the leaves and spin out silk for their cocoons. From the cocoons, machines spin thread.

"On the fourth floor they dye the thread — *purpura, rosa, amarillo, dorado, azul, azul marino, crema, café, violeta, naranja, bronce antiguo, siena palido, cascara de huevo, hueso—*"

"I think we get the picture," Mimi says. *"Vámonos!"*

"But you have only just arrived."

Mimi counts on her fingers: "Tell us about the fifth floor, sixth floor, seventh floor of that ramshackle building. Get on with it!"

"Okay, okay, *Apong bin.*"

Little Buddha giggles till his face flushes.

"What is it?"

Once he has calmed down, Little Buddha says, "Nothing."

"Tell me, Little B."

"Most naughty."

"Little B!"

Little Buddha stage-whispers in her ear: "Vagina face."

"From seventh to thirteenth floor, only looms," the young woman explains. Ranks of them, floor after floor, a woman or man hunched before each one. Children crouch next to them brandishing turbo squirt guns. Every 30 seconds or so the weavers get a blast of water on the chest or back: their soaked white garments shine translucent in the sun.

Briony joins the passengers in laughing at the carefree spraying.

"It's like something out of *Modern Times*," Mr. Dilman Chaphand of Old Greenwich, Connecticut, calls out.

"And the roof," Taffy Bentworth, Oregon pressed-wood matriarch wants to know, "what are the people doing on the roof with those silver cans?"

"Tiffin," the guide answers carelessly, sure this is something everyone must know.

"Lunch," Mimi says. "It comes in those silver tins."

Briony focuses on the diners' hands. "Some sort of stick food, like *yakitori*."

The young woman brightens. *"Exactamente!* But worms, not chicken.

"Silkworms?" Briony asks.

"Eww!" Most of the passengers turn away.

The silk guide claps her hands. Twenty or more young girls, all in glittering *cheongsam,* spin into the room, each flourishing a gleaming length of silk.

"Oh!" the passengers cry, "Oh! Oh!" They hurry toward the dervish girls, desperately trying to touch the flying scarves. The girls, too quick for their old hands and frail arms, snatch them away at the last moment, dangling them above sun-blotched heads, teasing them round wizened necks and thickened waists before swirling them into the bright air, their giggles whishful as silk.

Intense glass clattering — Briony looks up. The chandeliers shake and chatter like wind chimes, and the sensation — once felt, never forgotten — that the floor has turned to gelatin: how an earthquake feels in an earthquake-proof building.

The passengers haven't figured it out yet, but the girls know. They go to the tour group as the great windows begin to warp and jitter, and guide them toward interior walls.

The entire tower trembles and swivels as if it's being screwed into the ground. The oldest passengers, too slow to make it to an interior wall, are soon ringed by young girls who ease them to the floor and lie down between them to stop the passengers from rolling. The chandeliers spin, eerily trilling, glass harmonicas of death.

"Safe!" cries the guide as she clings to Mimi and Little Buddha. "*Totalmente* safe!"

Rationally, Briony's sure they'll all be fine — she's been through shit like this before.

The building falters, squirms. If it were rigid, she realizes, it would snap like a Popsicle stick. But like a gargantuan metronome, it sways and bends to the seismic storm like bamboo.

Knowing this in no way diminishes her terror. She feels warmth streaking down her legs, filling her shoes. Only days ago she longed for death, but on her own terms, not as an abrupt victim of *force majeure*. Now she's all hopeful and urine-scented as the city of Modigliano cleaves down the middle: "I want to live!" a melodramatic voice inside her cries.

An old woman trembles next to her, as does the peacock feather in her fascinator. She looks down in dismay at the yellow puddle spreading round her court shoes. Following the girls' example, Briony wraps herself around the woman and they sink together to the slippery floor. Eye to eye, nose to nose, lip on lip, they pass the same shallow breath back and forth, Briony's teeth chattering, the old woman's false ones going clak-clak-clak.

Briony now feels less sure of their survival as the floor jerks and rolls them back and forth till they're soaked. Previous quakes she's known lasted only an eternal moment or two. This one seems to redouble its intensity every few seconds. She and the old woman are buoyed off the floor again and again, only to slam back down. Briony succeeds in rolling the old woman on top of her so she's spared the worst jolts. Oddly, the old woman's smiling. "I've wet myself," she whispers.

"Me too." They laugh like silly fools, so hard it takes Briony a few moments to realize the quake's force has waned — the chandeliers no longer spin and jabber but only rock to and fro, dinging.

The silk guide, not a hair out of place, extricates herself from Mimi and Little Buddha. *"Por favor,"* she calls out, "please to remain on the floor. It is not over."

But it seems to be.

A high electronic shriek rends the air.

"What is that?" Little Buddha asks.

"Alarme de terremoto."

"Earthquake warning siren," Mimi translates. "Right on time."

The old lady rolls off Briony, who helps her to her feet. They cling together unsteadily, though the tower seems almost stable now.

Briony reaches out to straighten the old woman's feather. "You're all right?"

"Shaken, not stirred," she says. "Thank you so much. I must go find my husband. Last I saw him he was on his way to the gents'. Too late for me!" The old woman laughs as she hobbles off.

"Look! Look!" A man in a pre-wrinkled écru linen suit hurries toward the window wall. "A miracle!"

The building across the way has survived the quake too, along with the workers in it, though a few of the squirt-gun boys and girls have rolled perilously close to the open windows. Weavers begin to stand and brush one another down, look for their friends or relations, and check their threads and looms.

The workers on the rooftop open their silver tins to resume their lunches, and Briony's struck once more by the resilience of people who live in Asian quake zones, their aplomb in the face of potential disaster. During the past turbulent minutes, no one screamed or behaved in a hysterical or unseemly manner.

Even now the young girls bring out bolts of multi-hued cloth to display on the glass countertops lining the walls. Even now the passengers, agitated but unbowed, stagger over to inspect the gorgeous wares, prepared to drive a hard bargain with girls who make 30 *shindos* a week.

Briony's about to ask the price of a scarf so diaphanous it's mainly air and light when the first aftershock arrives. The shelf cracks, the scarf floats down and then up in the air, unsure of the way to the rolling floor.

The workers' building appears to take this new jolt head on, weavers knocked from seats they've only just retaken, squirt-gun kids clinging to disintegrating walls or snapping pillars, rooftop tiffin cans ringing as they bounce and roll, women reaching out to draw child workers close.

The fourth, no, the fifth aftershock produces a grinding so dense Briony feels it creep up her back vertebra by vertebra until it tanks through her brain. Across the way, the fourteenth floor thuds down to the thirteenth, the thirteenth to the twelfth, the twelfth to the eleventh, like tiles slammed down in a rage by *mah-jong*-playing colossi.

A mass scream like that of crowds at a soccer game cheering a big goal that wobbles awry at the last moment, deflating the cry into a terrible sigh. Bodies rain down, alone or in conjoined pairs. The rooftop remains suspended as if levitating a moment or two. Then a new and racing tremor pitches the gravelled surface forward and down, tipping lunch parties into the yellow-dust clouds surging up to swallow them.

The *Emerald Tranquility* passengers, recent silky purchases in hand, had turned toward the windows at the first aftershock, the first screams. They stand transfixed by what they see so near and yet so insurmountably distant. Screams differentiate themselves now, calls of agony, terror, for help or deliverance. By the time the *palacio's* marble floor has finished its own safe, quavery roll, the other building has disappeared, covered over with a grimy blanket of black smoke rising from snapping flames. Where these clouds thin, they can see arms reaching up out of the rubble, twisted or bent like rebar. Bloody rebar.

In the slowtime notime aftertime of the quake, the only thing moving at speed is the first ambulance to arrive, followed by a second, third, and fourth, along with a convoy of larger vehicles — vans, trucks, and a dilapidated tank with large red Xs rather than crosses painted on their roofs.

Looking down, Briony realizes that, instead of heading for the dust-obscured wreckage teeming with the injured and dying and their broken chorus of pain, the vehicles have come to a halt at the duck-crowded base of the *palacio*.

"Help is on the way," the guide calls out to everyone. "Help is on the way."

The passengers make for the curving glass and try to signal the men in beige uniforms unloading gurneys, oxygen tanks, and defibrillation machines that they've got the wrong building. Some of the men look up at them and wave or give enthusiastic thumbs-up.

Mimi and Little Buddha usher everyone toward the stairway next to the elevators. "Stay calm, everyone," Mimi calls out. "Do not attempt to use the elevators. That's the most dangerous thing you can do."

"Muchas gracias," the silk guide says, tears coursing down her cheeks. "Thank you for your visit to *Palacio de Patos Blancos. Vayan con Dios."*

She spits on the marble floor.

Rescuers stream in from the stairwell. Two of them grab Mimi and try to force her onto a gurney, while a third claps an oxygen mask onto the guide.

"We are fine." Taffy Bentworth points to the curving window and the calamity beyond. "Go and help those poor people over there." One of the larger rescuers hoists her over his shoulder and disappears down the stairwell. The remaining passengers are hustled or carried after them, many already fitted with IV lines and aluminum stands swinging plastic bags of a neon-orange fluid.

Little Buddha shouts at the men. "What are you doing?"

"These people are not hurt," Mimi tries to explain

to a small man in a purple beret approaching with defib paddles. "Go next door!"

A bespectacled man with Gucci stripes on both shoulders turns to Little Buddha. "You are leader?"

"I am leader!" Mimi shouts in his face.

Giving her a cursory glance, he turns back to Little Buddha. "First we take esteem guests to hospital. We come back soon, take dogs."

"Dogs?" Mimi cries.

Little Buddha speaks at length with Colonel Gucci in a language Briony doesn't recognize.

"'Dogs,'" Little Buddha explains, "is the affectionate term the Modiglis use for the lowest caste."

Mimi grabs the officer by his stripes. "We are not going to hospital. We are not injured. Our coaches are down in the parking lot. We will board those coaches and return to our ship immediately. Do you understand?"

Colonel Gucci salutes Little Buddha. "Yes, sir!"

For a measureless time Briony and the others stare down but see very little. At last a handful of rescuers disappear into the noonday dusk. The sound of their boots on marble, then rubble, reaches the passengers along with muffled noises no one would wish to decipher.

The ground lurches once more, and once more again. Briony, Mimi, Little Buddha, and the few remaining passengers fall to their knees or backsides. From far below them come ponderous shifting sounds, along with an unutterable odour.

The old lady in the peacock fascinator, on her back once more, sees them first and points: above the smoke and flames, beyond the toxic clouds that make them all gasp and weep, a trio of broad-winged raptors silently circle. More and more come to join them, swirling the hazed sky.

One dives into the maelstrom, then another and another. It is so neatly done, Briony thinks as she watches, with such precision, each bird patiently awaiting its turn. From the veiled wreckage can be heard their rackety, screeching cries.

DINNER AT THE Murmuring Mermaid Bistro is a subdued affair — a number of diners push away their *jamon iberico pata negra de bellota senorio* starters without lifting a fork. The waiters too look downcast as they bring in the *ris de veau* with baby carrots, shiitake mushrooms, and ginger, most of which Briony's tablemates only toy with, few capable of taking more than a bite or two.

When their server splashes dark rum into the indentation in the Bombe Alaska's meringue mountain and the blue flames dance, Mr. and Mrs. Lysander Spottington of Newport, Rhode Island, and Tangier excuse themselves and leave the room.

"I'm no expert in such matters" — Kurd waves a fork laden with plump thymus — "but I think there must be no building codes of any kind in all Modigliano."

"How can you say that? You were not there." Mimi's countersunk eyes brighten momentarily. "The building *we* were in withstood the quake quite nicely."

"It translated the shocks into waves, for the most part," Briony says.

"It must have been awful for you." Teenah places a warm hand over her cold one.

"Clearly the building that collapsed was constructed to no code at all," Mimi says. "Everything about it was haphazard and improvised. Even the bougainvillea vines growing up the walls — when I commented on their beauty, the silk guide told me they were plastic."

"Do we know yet how many persons were sadly killed?" Kurd asks between bites.

"They're still counting. Nearly everyone, I gather. Hundreds and hundreds." Mimi studies her untouched plate. "Those not crushed to death were burned alive."

"Who is responsible?" Teenah asks. "Who owned this terrible building?"

"What does it matter," Little Buddha says, "who owns the building? Which American and U.K. fashion companies have their silk made here? All the workers are dead — there is nothing to be done." He gently traces a tear trickling down Mimi's left eye. "Your tears are for nothing, my naive and sentimental lady. Not all your piety and grief can cancel out a jot of their woe. They are most surely dead, dead and gone. The great ship sails on!"

"That is so heartless, Little B," Mimi says, "even for a Buddhist."

"Not heartless." Kurd tucks into his singed dessert. "The way of the world. Bring in new laws, new regulations, higher wages for workers, better safety inspections, tighter codes, outlaw baksheesh and backroom deals, replace the corrupt government — Western owners will simply close shop and relocate to a more open-market country without such fastidious oversight. I see this happen so many times in my work."

"So we must abandon the dead to their deaths?" Teenah leans to one side for the waiter to refill her glass of Screaming Eagle Cab.

"Madame Rehbinder has already set up an offshore fund to compensate the families of the deceased — everyone's chipping in," Mimi says. "The London office of Deloitte Accounting, Consulting, and Secreting has already determined a fair market price for the deceased."

"How much do the dead go for now?" Teenah thumps down her glass so hard ruby gouts dot the damask.

"Exactly $2,067.35. Quite a generous evaluation considering the current state of the Modigli economy. Also, $352 for loss of limb, vision, hearing, disabling spinal injury, or related prosthetic costs."

"Admirable!" Kurd helps himself to Teenah's untouched dessert. The meringue gives him a ghostly moustache. "I am only meaning this in the most ironic way, you see."

"Fuck your irony!" Teenah makes to fly from the table, but the tablecloth clings to the *fil d'or* latticework of her ribbed-silk peplum. She untangles it and storms off.

Briony feels untouched by her histrionics, recalling the Tri family's wide holdings in textiles.

"How I love her fire." Kurd stands. "I must go solace her at once. She takes these things so personally."

"Imagine that." Briony pushes back her chair too, but the sweetbreads lie so heavy in her belly she can't quite achieve a dramatic exit equal to Teenah's.

9

THE NEXT MORNING SHE finds Mrs. Moore in the Leviathan Lending Library in a velvet wingback chair — filtered sunlight haloes her silver hair — reading Svevo, a name that almost means something to Briony.

Briony stands before her like a fool and waits for her to look up. She's prepared to stand there forever in her *Tadasana* pose, all barren cliffs and *prana* breathing. But Mrs. Moore won't acknowledge her: she turns a page and, seven Briony breaths later, turns another. Yet how satisfying to be upright and focused — wholly ignored while furtively embraced by such fierce inattention. At first it feels like a kind of combat, and soon only a soft siege. Mrs. Moore's breathing, her turning pages, Briony's straining heartbeat, the faint click at the back of her throat when she swallows.

Mrs. Moore lifts the book from her lap and, holding it open before her like a chorister, reads out: "'I tried to silence the youth, saying the light was certainly sad because we could see all the things in the world.'"

She closes the book and hands it to Briony spine first: *Confessions of Zeno*. "It may help. Probably not."

"But you're not finished."

"I've read it before. I would call you by your name except I've forgotten it, assuming I ever knew it. The tango girl."

"Briony. I was afraid you wouldn't remember me."

"The body knows what the body knows. The mind, well, the mind" — she smiles — "knows less than nothing."

The book feels cool and slight in her hands.

"You've come looking for me before."

"Yes."

"But today for a different reason."

"Yes."

"You were there yesterday, at the event."

"Yes."

"And you wish to tell me about it?"

"Yes."

"Unfortunately, I'm old enough to say I can't listen any longer. I've made up my mind. Another story, another disaster — another serving of other people's suffering will not change it. I am past sated. The world sees these things every day, you know this, some from a closer vantage point that others. But seeing changes nothing. Telling changes nothing."

"It feels like it could."

"Because you, my dear, are having a poignant reaction. You feel that because you've witnessed their pain you've also somehow shared it."

"Maybe."

"This is a confusion of categories. You're experiencing distress over the sight of their pain, not the pain itself. This is not particular to you. No matter how hard we try, we can never quite imagine the pain of others. We only look on and try to diminish its impact on us, tame it any way we can so as not to be overwhelmed by it. We struggle to make it fit the safe proportions of our own lives. We too have suffered —*peines d'amour,* the heartbreak of mourning a loved one, the anguish of never having everything we need to begin to live a full life — a different scale and key. Compared to theirs, our pain isn't worthy of the name. Invidious, don't you think, even to place them side by side?"

Briony studies the old woman in silence for a long time, having expected so much more from her, Briony's own desires inchoate yet all tied up in love and longing and her need for sympathy and consolation. In bringing Mrs. Moore this story she feels like a cat dragging in a little savaged mouse in search of approbation from her mistress.

She had thought the pain she feels for others, the pain she brings to Mrs. Moore, would elevate her in the old woman's eyes. She would see Briony's compassion, the sensitive depths of her soul. Strange then that Mrs. Moore's mercilessness provides a different kind of comfort. She has so neatly contrived to remove Briony from the tragic equation altogether.

"The question is —" Mrs. Moore says. "No, let me begin again. There is no question. Can you think of even one?"

In her steady gaze Briony believes she can. "What am I to do with it then?"

"With what?"

"The story you won't let me tell."

"Try seeing it as something other than a story. Maybe it's not another step on your path from superficiality to redemption after all. As a story, you think it will change you, and perhaps it already has. But so what? Look at it as it is, not as a story but as the thing itself — no beginning, no end, but something always there that will be there forever, not so much recurring as ever in the process of being."

"Like *l'éternel retour?*"

"You've read your Nietzsche."

Briony blushes. "I do have a liberal arts degree."

"But no, not like Nietzsche at all. What you saw doesn't end and begin again and again. It isn't an ouroboros but more like the universe — or at least one of them — flat and open, all there all the time. We must imagine the infinite pain of the horizontal universe the poor inhabit alone.

"Over here we live in our nice spherical universe, both closed and finite. Occasionally our round universe spins so close to their flat one, we get a good long look before we safely rotate away once more. What you got yesterday was not a story but a boundless panorama of another, planar cosmos. Do you see what I mean?"

"No."

Mrs. Moore laughs aloud. Briony can see the dense gold nuggets of the crowns at the back of her mouth. "No matter. The nattering of an old woman."

Briony stares into her topaz eyes. "You don't think that at all."

"I like you, Briony. You're smart enough to catch a whiff of the truth while also understanding the entire odour of the world would destroy us both."

"You don't really know me. I'm more clever than smart."

"Allow me then to infer a complex mind, if not a profound one. Or maybe not so much complex as conflicted: a young woman in a vicious struggle with herself."

Mrs. Moore stands, swaying slightly as the roll of the ship catches her. "Now I must go to my cabin. Time for my morning nap."

She leaves Briony on the diagonal.

LUIS EMERGES FROM HER BEDROOM. "I have laid out on your bed two fashion choices for you: your grosgrain halter top and chain-mail leggings — very nice if you're going for a more casual look — but also, in case you are having the more formal feelings, the cascading isinglass gown with gannet-feather trim sprinkled with sun-bleached cowrie shells. You will go to Second Seating as usual?"

"No, Luis. I will go to no seating."

"What is wrong, *carita*?"

"I don't feel like dressing up tonight."

He places a warm palm on her brow. "No? You are not feeling well?"

"I'm not very hungry."

He takes her hand. "Something is wrong?"

She takes it back. "What do you mean?"

"You speak slightingly of fashion; you have no appetite. This is not the usual jolly Briony."

Jolly, Briony thinks. What is this, a P. G. Wodehouse novel? "The richness of ship life is getting to me, Luis. Rich food, rich clothes, rich people. I need a simple evening alone."

"But you must eat something. Shall I prepare you a light snack, maybe a nice cheeseboard and a small garden salad accompanied by a bottle of Billecart-Salmon Brut?"

"I've seen your cheeseboards — enough to feed a village. And I'm tired of champagne. It makes my nose fizz."

"Tired of champagne? Shall I call the ship doctor?"

"I don't feel hungry, okay?"

"I won't insist. If later in the evening you feel peckish, please dial room service. They are open 24 hours, you know."

"I promise."

He makes to go, then turns on his heel. "Am I obliged to worry about you, Miss Briony?"

She gives him her jolliest smile. "Not for a moment."

AT MIDNIGHT SHE GOES up to Lido Deck, where the pong of sunscreen hangs in the air. She contemplates the illuminated rectangle of the pool, chasing her thoughts as they chase her, a roundelay of self-recrimination and nascent hope. She knows herself to be the worst person in the world — superficial, uncaring, callous — but she has met a woman who may be able to help her with that. At the same time she understands if she pushes too hard, Mrs. Moore will disappear. The old woman tolerates her, but only just.

Earlier in the evening she read, or tried to read, *Confessions of Zeno*. Without Mrs. Moore's magisterial recitation, it turned out to be a banal little book about some Italian rich guy trying to juggle his mistresses and stop smoking at the same time. A summary judgement, she knows — she may have missed something.

She misses Mrs. Moore.

KURD HAS SPRAWLED ACROSS the chaise longue in Briony's suite, while Teenah perches on a pouf. How odd, she thinks; she can sit with them now and feel nothing: no desire for Teenah, no jealousy or dread of Kurd.

Kurd downs his snifter of artisanal mezcal in one go. Teenah only sips at hers.

"Are you hungry? I could order room service."

"*Ich habe sehr Hunger*," Kurd says. "What about you, Teenah?"

"I wouldn't say no."

"What will you have?"

Teenah considers. "Nothing gourmand, nothing special, nothing with foie gras, gold leaf sprinkles, or nasturtium petals."

"I'll have a large cheeseburger on a big bun, please," Kurd says, "with *fettig* fries."

"Fetish fries?" Teenah looks doubtful.

"What is this word in English? Not 'oily' but —"

"'Greasy'?"

"Wonderful, my Briony. A true writer always has the right word."

"What are you having?" Teenah asks.

"Oh, I had such a big dinner."

"We didn't see you in the dining room. Did you go to First Seating?"

She nods her lie.

"What did you have?"

"The *lapereau aux fines herbes.*"

"You are so lucky. I so love a good bunny. They did not offer this Second Seating." Kurd licks his lips with unseemly thoroughness.

Briony picks up the handset and waits for the customary ten seconds of Louis Armstrong burbling his catarrh. Nothing happens.

"They do not answer?"

"It's not even ringing."

"Please allow me to try." He punches the button repeatedly, staring at the handset in disbelief. "But what shall we do? I am this famished." He rubs his sunken belly.

"Let's see. I've got the perpetually replenishing box of chocolate truffles on the mantelpiece, today's — no, yesterday's now — cashew and macadamia nut bowl, the half-bottle of mezcal, and a bottle of Diplôme Dry Gin and one of Tanqueray."

"Both?"

"Tanqueray's for guests." She opens the fridge, its door disguised as a Louise Nevelson construction. "I've got three *tamago* from I don't know when — Tuesday's lunch?"

"I could manage a truffle or two," Teenah says.

The Lalique chandelier and wall sconces flicker, dim, burn bright once more but with a hint of ozone, flicker again, and finally fade to black.

"What the hell?" Briony says.

"I am sure this is nothing," Kurd announces. "A ship

of this size will have many, many auxiliary systems."

On cue, the lights come up again, but half as bright as before.

"You see, now the support generators work. There's nothing at all to worry about."

The in-room intercom sputters and squawks.

"Ist das Ding an?" Moist blowing sounds, followed by light thumping. "This is your captain speaking. Forgive me for perhaps waking you in the middle of the night. As those of you who are still up have surely noticed, the lights have gone dim. This is but temporary.

"There has been a small, really the tiniest of fires in the engine room. This has caused the main generator to disable herself. As you can see, we have — very smoothly, let me add — transitioned to our backup system."

"A fire in the engine room?" Kurd cries. "But this is most serious!"

Teenah takes his hand. "He did say it was very small."

"This they always do when disaster strikes: minimize. It is so like when an American president has been shot and the television says, 'He is resting comfortably, joking with his family.' But everyone knows this means he is truly on death's doorstop."

"'Doorstep.'"

"Thank you, fair Briony."

The captain goes on: "This most small emergency has meant we've had to seal off — only temporarily, of course — for our passengers' own safety Halston, Hummel, Anthracite, and Zircon Decks, which remain in complete darkness. If passengers on those decks will but quietly remain in their rooms, help will arrive soon, I assure you. Please, to avoid injury, do not attempt to move about in the darkness. Our crew, bearing small torches, will be with you soon."

"But Briony—" beads of sweat stipple Kurd's brow "—if it is only dark there, why must they seal off the lower decks?"

"The captain said it was for their own safety."

"Oh Teenah, will you believe everything you hear only because he is in authority? Something else must be wrong. What are they hiding? Or more to the point, who are they searching for?"

"You're so paranoid—" Teenah begins.

"We again assure you," the captain breaks in, "that all is under control. There's no need to—" A contained explosion crackles the intercom, followed by the sound of running feet and, possibly, small-arms fire.

Tap, tap, tap on the intercom. "Here is Tilong Sagamar, new first mate speaking. Captain Kartoffeln no longer available."

Long empty pause. Metallic whispers.

A different, raspier voice says, "Captain going to engine rooms so he solve small problem. No problem at all."

A third, high-pitched voice adds, "Nothing to alarm! Nothing to alarm!"

Louis Armstrong takes it from there: "'Sail away, sail away/We will cross the mighty waters—'"

10

DAWN'S BREAKING WHEN A pounding comes at the door.

Briony hauls it open. In tumble Mimi and Little Buddha.

"Bolt the door!" Mimi cries. "Bolt it now!"

"It is most all right, my Mimi." Little Buddha strokes her heaving shoulders. "Please control yourself. Remember your breathing."

"We don't know it's all right. We don't know anything!" she gasps.

"But does this not very much represent the truth of our human condition?"

"Praun, please, this is not a Buddhist teaching moment. We're in serious danger."

"What's wrong?" Briony asks. "Chocolate truffle?"

Little Buddha scoops up three before Mimi pushes the box aside.

"We must our strength upkeep."

"Perhaps a shot of something to fortify you both." Kurd reaches for the mezcal.

"Yes, indeed." Little Buddha snatches the bottle and pours a tumbler for himself and a shot for Mimi, which she refuses. He glugs down his, then hers.

"Please tell us what you know," Teenah says.

"A mutiny!" Mimi wails.

"A mutiny?" Briony, Teenah, and Little Buddha echo her.

"A mutiny!" Mimi confirms.

Briony thinks they sound like a demented chorus from *H.M.S. Pinafore.*

"It failed. Or we believe it failed. With the lower decks sealed off and still unsecured, who can be sure?"

"But who would mutiny —"

Teenah finishes for Briony: "— on a luxury cruise ship?"

"Captain Kartoffeln is such a dear and his crew are so loyal. I'm sure it's the fucking cleaners and below-deck workers who have fomented this," Mimi says.

"The ones who never see a lick of light?" Briony asks.

"Gang of malcontents. Always wanting something: a one-percent pay increase here, rubber gloves for everyone there, better below-deck ventilation. Why not silk sheets for all while they're at it?"

Kurd laughs. "I don't see how you can take this all so seriously. It sounds like high farce on the high seas. For a real mutiny there must be a real leader."

"There is, or there was. My sources tell me they were led by someone who's been with Emerald Cruises for years — Viktor Necterram in fecal sampling. He's the one who cut the fuel line that caused the engine-room fire. He was supported by a woman named Anna May Wang."

"Viktor!" Briony and Teenah say in unison. "Anna May!"

"You *know* them?" Mimi looks horrified by their close proximity to ship shit.

"We ran into them on the ship tour," Teenah says.

"I have also met Viktor." Little Buddha reaches for another truffle. "Capital fellow."

"He's a very nice man." Briony sees his tiny cabin, video monitor set to 3-D Tropical Rainforest.

"But imagine," Teenah says, "working with shit all day, every day."

"What do you think I do?" Mimi snaps. "Viktor and Anna May, as well as various stewards and one or two butlers, have been planning this all along."

"Not Luis?" Briony has to make sure.

"Who the hell's Luis?" Mimi says. "There is no one named Luis."

"Uh, my butler, Collins."

"Excitable little Latino guy with shaped eyebrows?"

Briony nods.

"Get real, Briony. Anyway, they somehow got hold of two of the Gummis' Micro-Uzis and stormed the bridge. The captain liquidated Viktor with his Luger, and the rest of his officers subdued the maids and stewards, but Anna May Wang escaped in the mayhem — we can't find her anywhere."

"Poor Viktor," Briony says without thinking.

"Poor Viktor!" Mimi turns on her. "Do you fully comprehend what he's done? What might have happened had he succeeded? If he'd killed the captain, or the fire hadn't been extinguished in a timely manner? This is no time for sympathy for a cold-blooded mutineer."

Briony tries to look contrite.

"With Anna May Wang still on the loose, and heaven knows how many sympathizers among the cleaners and laundry attendants, we're not out of danger yet. To make matters worse, the engineers are having difficulty restoring power to the lower decks, which must remain sealed off. The captain promised flashlights for passengers down there, but now it seems imprudent to send crew members to help until the lights are back on — too great a risk of ambush."

"People on those decks are still confined to their state-rooms?" Teenah asks.

Mimi nods.

"But what about food, what about the most basic accessories of life?" Kurd asks as Briony mouths "necessities" to him.

"Obviously, they'll be without food for the time being, and they've been advised not to use their toilets, which are temporarily non-functional."

"'Advised not to use,'" Briony says. "What if they have no choice?"

"They can either use their showers — those who still have running water — or the plastic dry-cleaning bags in their closets."

"Plastic bags!" Teenah cries out in horror.

"Oh, they'll be fine. It's only temporary. I predict everything will be resolved in short order. This is a tight ship. We've been through worse than this."

"You have?" Little Buddha asks.

Mimi wrings her hands. "Well, no. Not really."

"We must all practise patience and fortitude."

"Enough, Praun." Mimi heads for the door. "We have to get back to the bridge."

When they've gone, Briony picks up the handset and presses the room-service button again.

"'Sail away, sail away/We will cross—'"

She and Teenah and Kurd step out into the dim corridor. Funereal quiet. Three Gummis materialize at once, weapons drawn.

"Halt!" one of them shouts.

"'Halt!'?" Kurd mimics. "What must this be— *The Starship Troopers*?"

"Shouldn't you say, 'Who goes there?' first?" Teenah asks.

"Are we under lockdown too?" Briony says.

The largest of the Gummis—it was the little antsy one who cried "Halt!"—has a marble jaw and hayseed manner. "There's no rule, ma'am, but you're probably safer in your stateroom."

"But we are so hungry," Kurd protests. "We have had nothing to eat throughout this whole traumatic night long."

Briony and Teenah exchange glances. What trauma? What about the truffles, the limp sushi, all the macadamia nuts he scarfed down?

"I can't command you folks to go to your rooms," the big Gummi says.

Teenah looks hopeful. "Is breakfast still being served?"

"Only continental, ma'am, in the Bleu Pétrole Liquid Lounge on Chalamet Deck, until they get the electricals sorted out in the main galley."

"Will there be coffee?" Kurd cries. Trauma upon trauma.

"Not sure about that, sir—you'll have to ask."

"It is not as if an espresso machine consumes this much

energy." Poor Kurd, Briony thinks — no pout like an architect's pout.

"We'll leave you to it then." As the Gummis walk away, the little hyper one calls back, "Courage!"

"You go ahead," Briony tells Teenah and Kurd. "I have to check on something at Reception."

"Should you be walking about all alone, my brave Briony?" Kurd says.

Teenah scowls. "Oh please, Kurd."

"I won't be a moment."

"Courage!" Kurd calls after her.

She hurtles down a succession of clanking companionways until she reaches Atrium Lobby, where the bow-tied geezer at the glass baby-grand bowls through "How Deep Is the Ocean?"

The only person at Reception is, according to the dolphin-shaped name tag on his blazer, "GARTH." He's all of nineteen.

"Pretty quiet," she begins.

"You're telling me." His voice cracks on "me." He blushes.

"Must be really boring for you."

"Yeah, all the action's everywhere but here. At least I've got something to read."

She peers over the counter: a paperback copy of *War and Peace* that, judging from its puffy pages, at some point must have been fully submerged in a clear liquid not unlike water.

"Terrible about Prince Andrei."

"Sorry?"

"Prince Andrei? In the book?"

"I'm afraid I haven't gotten very far."

"It's so sad when he — but I don't want to spoil it for you, Garth."

"What may I help you with, miss?"

"Please call me Briony."

"Cool name."

She lowers her head becomingly. "Listen, I'm trying to locate a friend of mine, a Mrs. Moore. She's quite elderly and I wanted to make sure she's all right, but I can't remember what deck she's on."

"That's so thoughtful of you, Briony." Garth consults his monitor. "Let's see. She's in stateroom 28A down on Zircon Deck. Unfortunately, it's temporarily sealed off."

"Then I guess I'll just have to wait till they unseal it." She pats Garth's vaguely damp hand. "Thank you so much."

Zircon Deck? With Mrs. Moore's regal bearing and amethyst grapes, her mid-Atlantic drawl, Briony had assumed she was loaded, like nearly everyone else on board. Zircon Deck's where Gigot's tiny stateroom was as well.

Briony races back up to her suite to retrieve the flashlight tucked in next to the Bible, *Teachings of Buddha*, and the Qur'an in the drawer of her bedside table. It strikes her that steerage decks must not get flashlights along with their spiritual propaganda.

Reaching Zircon Deck, she's short of breath and short a plan. Four Gummis man the double doors leading to the staterooms.

"Can we help you?" the one with the cratered face asks, fingering the safety of his Micro-Uzi.

"That's okay. I was wondering how long the lower decks will be locked down."

The other men look equally agitated, like they're ready to kill and ask questions later. Former Chicago cops? The one with bad skin has a mouthful of gum he can't stop chewing and an eyelid tic that keeps on giving.

"That's for us to know," he says.

"Okay, then. Thanks a lot, gentlemen." She makes a fist and holds it high. "Courage!"

She does what they always do in movies: finds the nearest fire alarm, up on Fortuny Deck. She pulls down the bar. Nothing. Not terribly encouraging from a safety standpoint. She hurries along the passageway until she finds another, yanks on that — it comes off in her hand. Who knew the *Emerald Tranquility* was held together with kraft paper and duct tape? Seconds late comes a cochlea-shattering siren blast.

Running boots below her, running boots above, the almost soothing whirr of a single Micro-Uzi going off prematurely. She's betting on the dude with the rampant rosacea and the twitch.

The doors leading to Zircon Deck's staterooms stand open and unmanned. Blackness envelops Briony as she creeps along the corridor. She flicks on the flashlight for an instant to find she's at 16A. She feels her way from doorjamb to doorjamb and knocks softly on 28A. The fire alarm continues to blare, short pulses alternating with final trump blasts.

She hears a muffled voice within.

"Sorry?"

"Password."

"Seriously?"

"Password!"

She knocks more forcefully. "Mrs. Moore? It's Briony."

"PASSWORD!"

She hears Mrs. Moore's voice quite clearly. "It's all right, Evangelista. Are you alone, dear?"

"Yes."

"Well, then." The bolt slides, the security catch snaps back.

"Come in, come in," Mrs. Moore stage-whispers. A knot of grey-uniformed women huddle together on the double bed. Strong odours of sweat, smoke, chilies, and industrial-strength cleaning products make Briony's eyes water. "Ladies, this is my friend Briony. Briony, please meet Evangelista, Tuk-Tuk, Mercedes, Darna, Choum, Chit, and Izz.

"Hi, everyone!" Briony gives her best I-am-but-a-harmless-Canadian smile.

No one smiles back.

"Please sit down," Mrs. Moore says. The women shift to make room for her on the bed. "These ladies are members of an informal book club I've organized for the cleaners and other below-deck workers."

Not a book in sight. "An all-night book club?" Briony shouts to be heard over the fire alarm blasts.

"I'm afraid our readers got caught in the lockdown."

"What are you reading?"

"*The Wretched of the Earth*. Frantz Fanon." Mrs. Moore says without offering any evidence of the book itself. "Do you know it?"

"I've heard of it." So, more a cell than a book club. "You're reading it in English?"

Mrs. Moore looks startled. "In English? Not exactly. I read it in English and Evangelista translates it into—"

Briony stares at the women. "Thai? Tagalog? Vietnamese? Spanish?"

"Did you run the risk of coming here simply to interrogate us?"

Good point. "You must be starving."

"We're doing all right." Mrs. Moore opens the drawer of her bedside table to reveal a cache of Clif Bars nestled among the devotional tomes. "Would you like crunchy peanut butter? Chocolate brownie? I'm afraid the macadamia nut ones went rather quickly."

"I'm fine. I shouldn't stay."

Mrs. Moore nods. "You don't want to end up locked down with us, but I think you're fine for the time being. The Gummis are enthusiastic but undisciplined."

The bathroom door opens. Another young woman emerges, short and stocky in her swishing nylon uniform. "Esmiss Esmoor, hard to breathe in there."

"I'm sorry, Anna May. Come and meet my friend Briony."

She offers Briony a strong, chapped hand. "We meet before. At Viktor's."

Of all of them, she smells the most strongly of smoke.

"I heard you and Viktor started the engine-room fire."

"Lies! All lies! I cut the fuel line; Viktor brought Zippo."

"Anna May," Mrs. Moore says, "you needn't tell all the details to anyone who asks."

Anna May glowers at Briony.

"I really should be getting back."

Anna May steps in front of the door. "No! You stay here now."

"It's all right, Anna May. We can trust Briony."

Briony's not sure this is true but feels flattered.

"Briony," Tuk-Tuk says, "what kind of silly name is this?"

Mrs. Moore draws close to Briony and drills her with her eyes. "Isn't that right, Briony? We can trust you?"

"Yes," she tells them all. "You can trust me."

"Briony's on our side — aren't you?"

Briony has never been on anyone's side. From grade one gym class on, no one has ever picked her. Until now. "That's right, Mrs. Moore."

The fire alarm stops.

"Hurry off, my friend." Still shouting, Mrs. Moore pushes her toward the door.

"But —"

"But what?" She stands, arms akimbo, speaking normally now.

Briony whispers in Mrs. Moore's ear. "What will happen to you?"

"No need to whisper. We have no secrets in this room."

"You can't stay here indefinitely."

"We don't plan to. I'm simply offering refuge until the lockdown's lifted. Then my ladies can slip out and blend with the other workers. Except Anna May, of course."

Anna May snorts meaningfully.

"Passengers never know what their maids and cleaners look like." Mrs. Moore continues. "To them, they look like maids and cleaners — small, dark, ubiquitous."

"Maybe I can sneak back, bring snacks and things."

"It's far too dangerous."

"I'm beginning to see that. But I want to help."

Mrs. Moore smiles. "How you surprise me."

Looking as militant as possible, Briony raises her fist: *"No pasaran!"* The ladies get crazy giggles over her accent.

"Get out, get out." Mrs. Moore leans forward and kisses her. "Before you're caught."

Dazed by the touch of her lips, Briony slips out the door.

AT THE LUNCHTIME INFORMATION SESSION in the Broadway Melody Musical Theatre, Briony watches spellbound as Mr. Beauchamp De Groot, of the Antwerp blood-diamond dynasty, rails at Mimi, who, a swirl of saffron wrappings, looks ill-equipped to deal with the situation. "But when," he cries, *"when* will full power be restored? It is one thing to dine by candlelight, but to live by it is quite another matter. We are not in the court of Louis XIV. Furthermore, the champagne in my wine cooler has gone flat, and the butler informed me this morning there is no ice to be had on this *strontzak* ship."

"I want to assure you all," Mimi says, a slight quaver in her voice, "we are doing everything humanly possible to restore full power to the entire ship."

"What about my personal maid?" Mrs. Teal Spitz-Basenji of Fishers Island and Mustique wants to know.

"I didn't realize," Mimi says, "you'd brought along your personal maid."

"Of course I did — do you think I'd let just anyone tend to my most personal needs? Her name is Izz, she's about this tall and really quite quite brown. I sent her down at midnight to retrieve my dry cleaning because I wanted her to put it all on quilted hangers before she went to bed."

Mimi looks perplexed. "Her name is Is?"

"Izz!" Mrs. Spitz-Basenji replies. "I-Z-Z!"

"And her family name?"

"Family name?"

"You maid's last name."

"How the hell would I know? Ask my money man — he writes the cheques."

"My little Mademoiselle Maintenon hasn't been walked for hours and hours," the former Conservative Chancellor of the Exchequer, the Honorable Cosmo Briarley-Homp, calls out. "I've had my man paged again and again, but no response. The sitting room's Isfahan carpet looks a proper mess."

"Please, please." Mimi makes soothing motions with her hands. "If you can be patient only a little longer. As you can imagine, this is a very complex ship — it takes time to sort out all the problems that may arise from a power outage."

"Is that what they're calling it now — a power outage?" Count Guido Malodoroso (of Papal nobility) still wears his burgundy silk dressing gown at 17:50. "I hear there was some crazy mutiny."

"That's simply ludicrous," Mimi stammers. "Nothing could be further from the truth."

"I am told there was even the tragic loss of one life," Madame Rehbinder calls from a distant banquette.

"This is unfortunately true. One of our below-deck workers suffered a terrible mishap during the small engine-room fire." Mimi pauses. "He had been with Emerald Cruises for fourteen years."

"But this is too sad," Madame Rehbinder's voice thickens in sympathy. "When will be his funeral? We must make a collection to pay for a meaningful floral tribute. Poor fellow."

"There will be a memorial service for him once lockdown of the lower decks has ended. It's painful to report very little of him remains to bury."

"But I am thinking you said it was only this small fire," Count Malodoroso says.

"It was," Mimi nods, "but his polyester lab coat went up like" — she snaps her fingers — "*that*."

"All I wish to add," Mr. Beauchamp De Groot says, "is that it is a most terrible scandal that such events should occur on a ship of this quality and reputation. As soon as the exorbitant *weefee* is restored, I intend to alert the media about the depredations we have been forced to endure."

"Ah, ladies and gentlemen, our captain has finally arrived." As Captain Kartoffeln takes the microphone, Mimi whispers, "Where the hell have you been?"

He whispers back, too low for Briony to hear. All colour drains from Mimi's face.

"My dear fellow travellers, I'm sorry to interrupt this no-doubt important and most helpful information-giving session, but the first officer has alerted me that a powerful typhoon is headed our way. I am most confident we'll be able to outflank it, even on auxiliary power. In the meantime I commend you to the safety of your staterooms."

"But on so clement a day?" Madame Rehbinder says. "Why, not thirty minutes ago I was playing paddle tennis in the bright sunlight."

Passengers break for the theatre doors. Rain already spackles the wide lobby windows. Briony watches in silence as iridescent clouds churn and squirm like eels in a barrel.

11

ON THE GOLD-LACQUERED COFFEE TABLE Luis has laid out a roll of gaffer's tape, a small tin of Aspirin, an ornate pair of grape scissors, what looks like a nicotine patch, a bowl of chopped ginger, a small iron kettle, a blue teapot and two cups, a bowl of opium-poppy pods, a quartered lemon, a pyramid of brown-sugar cubes, and an alabaster mortar and pestle.

"What is all this?" Briony reaches for the kettle.

He slaps her hand. "These are all the best things for seasickness. Trust me, I know." He grabs the tape. "First we must tape your tummy."

"Oh, come on."

"No, really. Lift up the shirt, please."

"Luis!"

"Hurry, my Briony — before it is too late."

She tentatively reveals her midriff. He pops an Aspirin in her navel and seals it in with tape.

"This is supposed to work how?"

"We try a little everything, okay? Put on this bracelet."

"I'd rather die."

"What's wrong with it?"

"It's tacky."

"You hide it with your sleeve, or a nice *diamanté* cuff."

"I don't have a nice *diamanté* cuff."

"I am sure we will be able to find something in your pretty jewellery pouch, even if it is only paste." He holds up the bracelet to show her the green bead on the inside of the silver-plated band. "You see," he says as he settles it on her wrist, "the little bead will massage your P6."

"My what?"

"Holy acupression point inside your wrist."

"Right."

"Do not do this rolling of the eyes, please. You must believe or it won't work."

The ship tilts up, slams down. "Where do I put the nicotine patch? I don't even smoke."

"Behind your ear. It's a scopolamine patch to soothe the nerve fibres in the teensy room inside your ear. You may have a little dry mouth at first or maybe dizziness."

Just like my usual meds, Briony thinks.

With the pestle, Luis crushes a handful of opium-poppy pods in the mortar. He scoops the mixture into the teapot along with some ginger, four sugar cubes, and the juice of half a lemon and pours steaming water into the teapot and replaces the lid. "We let steep. In the bedroom I have laid out your sweating clothes."

"I never sweat and as a result have no sweating clothes."

"I have bought for you at the Viridian Galleria on Balenciaga Deck. I saved the receipt."

"I thought they only sold stuff with Swarovski crystals sewn onto them."

"Only the tiniest little crystal seahorse riding across the back of the sweating shirt. You will see."

"*Luis.*"

"Go and place them on you right now."

The entire stateroom heaves. Briony nearly joins in. Wobbling into the bedroom she finds the offending sparkly items laid out on the shot-silk counterpane, as if Liza Minnelli has died there.

"Are you dressed?" Luis calls from the salon a few minutes later.

"Hideously."

"Come drink your tea down."

It's almost not bitter, almost doesn't taste like ash and dung.

"You lie on your nice velvet sofa and I will put the music."

The ship lunges once more: bowls and devices skitter about atop the coffee table.

Music fills the room. If you consider pizzicato violins and Tibetan gongs music.

"Luis — not Enya."

"Little joke, Briony."

Something tranquil fills the room — Schumann? Schubert? One of those Romantic bangers.

A sweet, lucid dream envelops her.

Sometime later the sea rolls and bumps, rocks and shakes her — slaps her hard. *Slaps her?*

"Luis, what the fuck are you doing?" She can see he wants to get in one last clout.

He stands over her holding the brightest, yellowest, most noxious slicker ever — it reeks of rubber and mildew — and the kind of sou'wester hat only seen on tourists sailing the *Maid of the Mist* at Niagara Falls.

"Now you go outside."

"Outside?" The ship pitches forward, plunges. The teapot erupts, fragrant liquid flows everywhere. "You're insane."

"You go out on deck, yes? The real typhoon comes in thirty minutes, maybe more. You walk ten, fifteen minutes. Clear your head."

"Good luck with that—I haven't been this baked since we set sail."

"You will be all fine." He helps her off the sofa and straps her into the yellow prophylactic cocoon. "Ha! You look like the big banana."

"Thank you so much."

He manoeuvres her jaundiced bulk toward the door.

"Keep your eyes on the horizon. This reminds your tummy where normal is."

"What if my tummy and I get blown over the rail?"

"You will be perfect." He gives her a shove and slams the heavy door behind her. She hears the deadbolt slide.

SILLY HAT. She unties it and watches as it sweeps down from deck to deck. Rain lashes her face, soaks her hair. The glorious wildness of it all as the far-off sea digs canyons, forms mountains, then tears them down to build them up again. Promising the worst, great cliff waves flatten at the last second before splatting harmlessly against the hull. Low quiet ones prove more treacherous as they slide under and lift the *Emerald Tranquility* high into the liquid air, poise it there for a millisecond of weightlessness before smashing it down again.

Trying to catch up with this raucous gravity, she bends her knees to lessen the lurch, but her timing's off: before she can sink to it, the deck rises up to rap her kneecaps. Her teeth clack shut on the tip of her tongue — the taste of pennies, scarlet expectoration.

Assorted crew members, also in banana gear, attempt to race past her on whatever mission has brought them to Pucci Promenade Deck. They stagger-fall, zigzagging from rail to slippery handrail. One shouts out, "Better go back to your stateroom, miss!"

Like hell. Back inside with Luis, the typhoon was a terrifying unknown, but now she's in it — in at the edges — clobbered by wind, splattered by rain and seawater, it seems the most intoxicating thing ever. She wants to go above to have the full 360 Hyper-IMAX Dolby Atmos catastrophic experience. The stairs to Lido Deck wrestle her to the top. Where one wave clobbers her spine, another splats her face flat — they're coming from both directions now. But the wave in her face is salt-free and smacks of chlorine, clearly arising from the Poseidon Pool, where the water billows and bucks end to end, nervy stallion trying to kick his way out of the stall.

Water encircles her. A high wall has built itself up off starboard, yet its hastening toward her causes more exhilaration than panic, the world's tallest dance partner coming to sweep her away. This buoyant poppy-dream of engulfment keeps her teetering in place far longer than she ought to be. Not for nothing do they speak of an irresistible force.

As she clings to the rail, a figure swathed in white streaming towels emerges from behind the flapping cabanas — Winged Victory of Samothrace catches an epic wave. The gale shifts, terry wings swing forward, obstructing the figure's vision, and it smashes to the deck. Briony slips and slides in that direction, overshooting her destination several times before arriving at the writhing mass of waffle-weave.

"Are you all right?" she shouts into the towels.

Mrs. Moore's long face struggles to surface, red and laughing. "I'm fantastic!" she gasps. "Have you ever felt anything so sublime?"

Wind knocks Briony sideways, but the older woman catches her wrist in her strong grip.

"How did you ever make it up here?" Briony says.

"It's so bad below, the Gummis failed to maintain lockdown. I slipped past several at the rail spewing windward only to seconds later re-devour their own dinners."

Briony's ear rings after the gale slaps her cheek. "Are the book-club girls still holed up in your cabin?"

"Only the one."

"Sorry?"

"Only Anna May. I reckoned it was a good time for the others to return to their posts — they won't be noticed in the chaos."

Sputtering and coughing, they attempt to return to the companionway, but the squall flattens them as they inch their way down the deck's steep decline. As Briony's about to grab the stair rail, decline upends into incline: they slide back toward the hoicking pool.

Mrs. Moore yells something, but the storm's roar drowns her words. She points toward the frenzied cabanas, and Briony crawls after her. Canvas walls inflate and deflate around them.

The older woman drags her to an oblong steel-and-glass structure. They try to pry open the heavy doors but the fury at their backs seals them shut. Hanging onto the door handles, they ride the swell until the blast shifts, tearing away most of Mrs. Moore's towels. Briony heaves one of the doors a quarter open and they squeeze in before the storm slams it, trapping Mrs. Moore's last towel between wet and dry.

They find themselves vacuum-packed, shut off from all mayhem. No roar or squall but the silent one — sea crags assault the floor-to-ceiling windows. Not even the rattle of hard rain makes a sound against the triple-glazing.

Briony's aware of another more mellifluous noise. A woman's amplified voice, melancholy, cloying, sings of honey, the lyrics making the obvious point that it's sweeter than wine.

"What the hell is this?" Briony struggles out of her stinky slicker.

Mrs. Moore shivers in her silver bathing suit. "I cannot remember who it is, some '60s folksinger from an art film about a girl pregnant out of wedlock and I forget what else. Before your time."

"Thank god." Hulking gold chairs and turquoise lamps like dwarf lighthouses range across the room's wide azure carpet of watery design. Reconnoitring behind the curving bar, Briony finds small towels and a stack of gold-brocade tablecloths.

She towels Mrs. Moore off as best she can, draping a stiff tablecloth around her until she's a dowager empress freshly escaped from the Forbidden City.

"Much better." Mrs. Moore's teeth clack together. "Wrap yourself up too, Briony. Your lips are blue."

"What is this place? I didn't even know it was here."

"The Sea-Change Lounge."

"Looks like a mid-century modern mortuary."

"An exact copy of a famous Los Angeles nightclub of that era, I was told."

Briony surveys the circular marble dance floor with its black and white swirls, like a hypnotist's revolving disc. "People actually dance here?"

"It's most often used for afternoon tea."

"I could do with something stronger than tea." She slips behind the bar again, where prismatic bottles line the shelves. "What do you fancy?"

"Brandy, large."

Snifters in hand, she guides Mrs. Moore to a pair of chairs facing the glass wall where the sea flings its worst.

She's about to settle into the chair on the left when Mrs. Moore beckons her to join her. "We will warm each other up," she says.

Oh?

She opens her brocade to Briony, who, sliding in next to Mrs. Moore, finds her naked. Damp hair against Briony's neck, bare breast touching her shoulder — only the one, beside a waxen strip of scar tissue.

With a start, Briony realizes she's imagined this moment for some time but always dismissed it from her mind, thinking, What must it be like to touch an old woman? followed by slight revulsion.

Here it is now, a crepe pouch barely filling her hand.

"I don't..." Mrs. Moore begins.

"Don't what?"

"Feel desire."

"Your nipple sings a different tune."

"My body responds — naturally. No preventing that. My mind, though, remains unaroused."

"I should stop?"

She shakes her head. "Just don't expect too much from me."

"I see."

"It can't be helped."

"I wonder."

"Each new girl thinks she'll be the one who breaks through, that tired old romance of unresponsive object combusted by the right knowing touch."

Looking down, Briony sees her pubes are sparse and white. She runs her fingers through them. Corn silk.

"If you're going to do that —"

"Yes?"

"Wet your fingers. I'm a dry old thing."

Briony spits in her hand. "Better?"

Mrs. Moore sighs. "But do not think you will be..."

"What?"

"You're making me lose my train of thought."

"Take your time."

"Don't for an instant think you'll be the one."

"The one?"

"Who will finally connect." Mrs. Moore's eyes roll back, her silver head subsides on Briony's breast.

Briony touches her brow. "You seem to swoon."

"I can see how it may look like that." Her words arrive slightly muffled by Briony's flesh. "If you truly knew my mind, its steely detachment..."

"Who cares about your fucking mind?" Briony withdraws to wet her fingers once more, though Mrs. Moore seems less dry than before.

Her head comes up. "You don't?"

"Not really."

Her eyes are alert, all else languid, deliquescing. "No one can truly touch me."

Briony's hand swims, turns, flashes. "Whatever."

A strangled cry.

It's gone all cramped, her hand. Briony can hear her own cry of pain, far away.

The old woman dead in her arms.

Sometime later Mrs. Moore reconfigures herself against Briony, who tries to slide out her numbed hand.

"Stop!" Paroxysms rack Mrs. Moore's body.

They sleep.

She awakens to Mrs. Moore hovering over her, eyes bright, smile placid. Briony sees Mrs. Moore has reset to her impermeable self.

"That was fun!" she announces. "Now we need to get back to our lives."

Fun?

The folksinger croons about how someone's left her tedious cake out in the rain.

. . .

THE TYPHOON HAS ABATED by the time the pair reach
Briony's suite. Briony guides Mrs. Moore into the bedroom and, tugging off the brocade tablecloth, sits her
down on the bed to give her a thorough towelling off.
Mrs. Moore winces at one point during her ministration,
and Briony realizes some tensile strength has gone out of
her. Mrs. Moore feels fragile, nearly frail. Briony takes
her dressing gown and wraps it round the older woman.

"You really are too kind," Mrs. Moore says from her
other, locked-off universe. "But I mustn't stay."

"Where will you go?"

"Back to my stateroom, to make sure Anna May is
all right."

"Seriously? No water, no power, no food, and you're
going back?"

"I must take her something to eat."

"How will you even get there? I'm sure the Gummis
are back at their posts by now."

"I will show them my electronic key."

"And then what?"

"Anna May and I will continue our work."

Briony can't stifle her laughter. "Your book club?"

"After a fashion."

"But don't you think —"

Pounding at the door. Briony steps out of the bedroom,
pulling the door closed behind her.

She drags open the door to her suite. A damp, dis-
arrayed Mimi tumbles in.

"Did you hear the news?" She takes in Briony's sequined sweats, her still-dripping, seaweed hair. "Have you been out in this mess?"

"What news?"

"Full power to be restored within the hour. The chief engineer and his team have been working full out to get this ship up and running again."

"Great."

"Soon lockdown will be lifted on the lower decks and we can start getting back to normal."

"After this, Mimi, what can normal mean?"

"Not sure I follow."

"Pirate attack, beheaded balaclava guys, Gigot kidnapped, hundreds dead on a silk excursion, insurrection — a whole world of chaos erupting. You suddenly call normal and think everything will fall back into line?"

"It's all been taken care of."

"Yes?"

"The miscreants have been apprehended and are now in the brig, where they can do no more harm."

"I didn't know there was a brig."

"Oh yes, quite a capacious one, thank goodness."

"How can you be sure you've got them all?"

"They were all part of the same group, hanging out in a passenger stateroom. We caught one as she tried to cut the line at the continental-breakfast buffet. She ratted out the others in short order. Well, a few renegades are still out and about, but we'll have them soon enough. We're still trying to locate the sympathetic passenger. Someone from the steerage decks, naturally. Zircon."

"She can't have gone far."

"'She'? I don't believe I indicated the passenger's gender."

A loud buzzer sounds close by.

The suite lights go up full. Mimi and Briony stand together blinking at their brilliance.

Mimi's turning to go when a muffled explosion erupts from beyond the bedroom door.

"What on earth?"

Briony beats her to the door and throws it open. No sign of Mrs. Moore, but a rank, palpable odour emanates from the bathroom.

"I wouldn't if I were you." Mimi places her hand over Briony's as she starts to turn the crystal doorknob.

Against her countervailing pressure, Briony gives the knob a twist, at once wishing she hadn't. The mirror-lined walls, the sarcophagus bath, the porcelain sink — all striated with excrement, the golden marble floor black with ooze, sink and shower drains gurgling with it.

Mimi shoves her back into the bedroom and yanks the door shut. "Only temporary," she shouts. "Just a glitch. Call the cleaners!"

She runs from the bedroom. The penthouse door thuds shut.

Mrs. Moore emerges from the walk-in. "Bigger than my whole stateroom in there. Pee-ew, we must get out of here."

As they clamber down the exterior stairs, a barrage of discrete explosions accompanies them from the other staterooms.

"Shit fireworks!" Briony shouts to the foul winds.

"Briony, do be quiet."

"We're going back to your place?"

"Where else? You heard the lady — the girls are in the brig. We could liberate them if only we knew where the brig is."

Briony wonders how she came to be involved in a girl-on-girl prison flick.

CONTRARY TO EXPECTATIONS, the Gummis aren't at their post at the entrance to Zircon Deck. As the pair head along the darkened corridor, the foul miasma that's dogged them during their descent dissipates. Mrs. Moore's stateroom hardly stinks at all.

Briony opens the bathroom door. "Immaculate."

"It didn't explode."

"Or has yet to."

"You will obviously have to stay here with me until your place is cleaned up." She doesn't look delighted at the prospect, but Briony's pulse races.

"I promise to keep to my side of the bed."

Mrs. Moore looks at Briony steadily. "Wisecracking all the way? It's not you, you know — honestly. I knew early on I wasn't suited for cohabitation."

"You were fine with a roomful of cleaners."

She laughs. "Far better a horde than one single other. I can tolerate anything but intimate attachment."

"You were doing pretty well up in Sea-Change Lounge."

"That was sex."

"Seemed like more at the time."

"It often does. It was nice."

"Nothing more than that?"

"I've always been able to separate emotion from sex. Otherwise one can end up in the most awful mess."

"I thought that was the whole point."

"Briony, you're young and have the stamina for that sort of thing."

"Don't patronize me."

Mrs. Moore's face is serene, her voice calm, but why does she look so trapped?

"We are two different people."

"Ya think? You don't usually speak in clichés."

Her eyes go dark and hard. "I have had a lifetime of people trying to make me feel what they feel."

In her voice Briony hears her own — the anxious edge whenever someone attempts to breach her territory. Yet here she is so eager to storm Mrs. Moore's. "I'm not one of those people. I want to be better than that. I promise not to coerce you into anything."

"You *are* better than that. You're my friend."

"What an upgrade."

Briony starts to leak and stream. Projectile tears spring from her eyes, ping off her arms and hands. How humiliating, she thinks. How broken and vulnerable.

Instead of moving to console her, Mrs. Moore steps back. Briony finds this reasonable. Who would want to be infected by such repulsive melancholy? This gross emptying out has never happened to her before, not even as a miserable child. If it ever does cease, she wonders if anything will be left of her—a damp spot on the wall-to-wall and the faintest scent of despair.

It does stop, as abruptly as it began. Briony still here as Mrs. Moore is still there, facing her with imperturbable eyes.

Briony's let herself go, allowed all she's hidden for a lifetime to pour out, hoping her vulnerability would draw Mrs. Moore closer to her. What an idiot—to reveal so much and receive nothing in return.

She feels a flash of hatred toward the old woman. Yet she knows Mrs. Moore has been honest with her, has stated her own position without ambiguity. It's not whether she loves her or doesn't. Far more simple than that: she's unavailable and intends to remain so. This is how it has always been for her, and nothing Briony does will alter that.

Mrs. Moore inspects her closely, wary of another outburst.

"Finished?"

Briony nods.

Mrs. Moore slips into the bathroom and returns with a handful of tissues. "Mop up." She puts a cool hand to Briony's brow. "Goodness, your hair." She pushes a few soggy strands behind her ears. "We have to get you out of that ridiculous track suit. I'm sure I can find something more appropriate. We have work to do."

12

THE SEA DISPLAYS CALM INNOCENCE, as if it's never heard of a zephyr, let alone a typhoon. Briony and Mrs. Moore reconnoitre Zircon Deck in matching white linen tunics. Not a sign of a Gummi anywhere, although they hear stomping boots and surly bellowing somewhere above. The terrible stench recurs now they're in open air. At least there are no more explosions. On the uppermost decks, passengers stand at the railings, handkerchiefs or blue surgical masks half-obscuring their faces.

Mrs. Moore holds up her hand and tilts her head to one side. "You hear that?"

"What?"

"Precisely. No engine hum or throb, no vibration at all. The auxiliary system's finally down too. We are adrift."

They look down the ship's flank: no wake, not even froth, only the slow slap of seawater against the hull.

"What does this mean?"

Mrs. Moore smiles. "It means that even with so many already in the brig, the other workers have succeeded in incapacitating the ship."

"I had no idea the mutiny was so widespread. Is the whole crew in on it now?"

"Not everyone, Briony, but enough. If you had to live

with four others in a tiny cabin far below the waterline, wouldn't you rise up too?"

"You've been so supportive of them—Anna May and the others."

"I don't simply support them. Don't you see? This is my fourth *Emerald Tranquility* South China Sea cruise this year. I've been organizing the ship, step by step. You can't hope to foment this kind of action out of nothing. So much groundwork has to be laid, so much preparation and recruitment, setting up a system of cells so word doesn't get out."

"You're organizing this for who?"

"'Whom.' Why, for them, my dear."

"I mean, who—whom—do you work for?"

"I just told you: for them."

"But who hired you to do this?"

"No one hired me. It was my idea, my plan, my organizing and execution. Something I've always dreamed of doing. One pure gesture to capture the world's eye."

"We're pretty far from the world's eye."

"Once the distress signal goes out—a ship full of some of the richest people in the world, stranded in their own shit and piss—don't you imagine attention will be paid?"

"Yes, certainly, but—"

A shriek of feedback, followed by Mimi's bull-horned voice issuing from on high. "Attention! Attention! All passengers please rendezvous on Lido Deck at once. Be sure to take the exterior stairs, as they remain"—more feedback squawks and sputters—"relatively uncontaminated. Attention! Attention!"

It's a long way up to Lido Deck, but Mrs. Moore leads the way at a clip. Briony trails behind, panting. She spots Madame Rehbinder in a pink caftan stained about the hem, helping old Major Chelmsworth Cholmondeley, who's trying to find purchase on the slick stair treads with his malacca cane. Mrs. Moore skirts past them calling, "Sorry, so sorry." At Limoges Deck, they're met with the sad sight of His Serene Highness Amondochan "Buddy" Thimerosol taking leave of his wheelchair-bound mother, her pale silk robe a slimy ruin, before he begins his upward climb. Mrs. Moore brushes past them too, nudging Buddy out of the way.

Saffron veils billowing about her, her bare feet mottled with grit, Mimi rushes up as Briony and Mrs. Moore step onto Lido Deck. "I've been so worried about you, Briony. Little B and I went to your suite, but you weren't there."

"Mrs. Moore was kind enough to let me stay in her stateroom."

Mimi gives Mrs. Moore a penetrating once-over. "I don't believe we've met."

"I'm afraid I haven't been terribly social this voyage. My sciatica, don't you know."

"Which deck are you on?" Briony can see Mimi registering their immaculate tunics. "Why, you must be on Zircon, Anthracite, Hummel, or Halston, since they were spared the explosions and eruptions."

"No shit on us," Mrs. Moore says graciously.

"What-ho, what-ho!" Little Buddha bustles up, pudgy cheeks smeared with a black viscous substance.

"Downwind, Little B," Mimi whispers.

He bows to Briony and Mrs. Moore. "Such a pleasure to see you." He turns back to Mimi and stage-whispers, "I cannot discover him anywhere."

Mimi blanches.

"Can't discover who?" Briony asks.

"'Whom,'" Mrs. Moore says.

"Shh!" Mimi draws them closer. "The captain—he's nowhere to be found." She turns back to Little Buddha. "Did you check the morgue fridges?"

"They are most full to bulging, my kumquat, but no captain. A fair number of Gummis seem to have gone missing as well."

Mrs. Moore gives Briony a triumphant look. "It's all coming down."

Other passengers finally straggle onto Lido Deck, many of them breathing hard or coughing thickly. With compassionate dexterity, Madame Rehbinder eases Major Chelmsworth Cholmondeley onto a sunbed.

"What on earth do I tell them?" Mimi's a picture of panic.

"I am sure the captain is perfectly safe." Mrs. Moore displays the smug smile of someone with inside information.

"You are?"

"The mutineers—" Mrs. Moore begins.

"Please don't call them that."

"Can you think of a better term—insurgents, rebels, renegades?"

"I consider them terrorists," Mimi whispers through clenched teeth.

"Of course you do," Mrs. Moore says. "You are American, after all."

"And what are you?"

"I am a citizen of *nulle-parte*."

"Huh?" Mimi's frantic eyes dart about.

Little Buddha looks dazzled. "You too?" he murmurs to Mrs. Moore. "I also am *apatride*."

Mimi looks perturbed. "Speak English, Little B."

"Stateless. I have no country, not since the so-called Chomp Chomp Hawkers' Centre riot in '97 back home. Ha! I was not even in town."

"You must say something." Briony gestures toward the sun-blasted crowd forming around them. "You asked them here."

Truly, they have arrived in numbers — the halt and the lame, the deaf and the barely sighted, the confused and the clearly demented — all looking smaller now, sullied and diminished by recent events.

Hereditary Grand Duke Basil-Haakon of the Mediterranean island tax-haven Plethoria waves a not-quite-spotless towel from the swimming pool's far edge. "Do you think, dear lady, we could get a drink before the proceedings begin?"

Mimi puts her bullhorn aside and addresses the crowd: "It's already taken care of. Waiters should be along any minute now. I should warn you though — we're momentarily out of ice."

"No ice?" the cry goes up. "How can we be expected to live like this?"

"People, people," the Hereditary Grand Duke calls out, "is this what we have come to? Surely we can rough it a bit until help arrives. It can't be long."

"*How* long?" a woman in a towering black wig asks. "This morning I called room service repeatedly and no one ever answered."

Mimi holds her hands up for silence. "Please! The *Emerald Tranquility* apologizes for these unfortunate happenings and understands your pain and frustration. But things are being put right even as we speak. Cleaners are now working hard on every deck."

"I haven't seen a goddamn cleaner in two days," a woman in a soggy muu muu yells out. "And you call this a luxury cruise ship!"

"If we could please keep this discussion civil," Mimi says.

"Fuck that!" the woman shouts back. "We're tired, we're filthy—all I had for breakfast was a cucumber sandwich with the crusts *still on*."

"At least you had breakfast," Hereditary Grand Duke Basil-Haakon reminds her.

"Please stay calm," Mimi says, "so you can hear my good news."

"I've lost my little Cordelia," a plaintive voice sounds from over by the cabanas.

"My friends," Count Guido Malodoroso says, still in his burgundy silk dressing gown despite the heat, "let us hear what dear Miss Mimi has to say."

"Help is on its way," Mimi shouts. "The captain has radioed for assistance."

A feeble cheer goes up.

Mrs. Moore catches Briony's eye and whispers, "Not true—how can the captain radio for anything if he's missing? Besides, we've thoroughly compromised all the comm systems."

"But where is the captain?" Doña Cuantos Cuantos-Besos says. "Surely it is he who should be telling us this."

Mimi can't conceal her agitation. Her hands wave about ineffectually, her voice pipes and cracks. "As you can well understand, Captain Kartoffeln's extremely busy. He has asked me to speak on his behalf."

"What nonsense!" Mrs. Moore's sharp voice slices the air. "The captain's gone missing and no one knows where he is."

"How dare you?" Mimi's face blanches with rage.

"Why not tell the truth for a change?" Mrs. Moore continues, "Most of the Gummis have been subdued in one way or another, the captain's being held in an undisclosed location, and you, ladies and gentlemen, are smack in the middle of a full-scale mutiny."

Total silence. A desolate voice calls out, "Cordelia!"

With much scraping of sunbeds the passengers labour to their feet.

"What utter nonsense!"

"Why, my wife and I saw a Gummi on our way here."

"This is outrageous!"

"Who is this ridiculous old woman in her white robe?"

"Some kind of cult!"

Mimi wields her bullhorn once more. "Do not listen to her." The device clicks and stutters, fails. "She doesn't know what she's talking about."

Next to the paddle-tennis court, the four sets of elevator doors glide open — Briony guesses there must still be enough power to keep the hydraulic elevators running—and out stream the maids and cleaners, laundry attendants and food servers, chefs and cooks and kitchen crews.

But not in their customary crisp uniforms. Instead they parade in mufti, though not their own mufti. A marabou-trimmed bed jacket's flung over the shoulders of a tiny young woman in shiny, thigh-high boots. A plump middle-aged woman wears a gold-beaded gown several sizes too small for her, and looks all the more regal for it. A tall, sun-wizened man of indeterminate age—Briony thinks he may be a butler—sports a purple velvet smoking jacket and red tartan golf trousers. A majestic woman in an immense jewel-laden turban and a puce silk opera cape sashays forth.

An assortment of coronets and diadems grace a quintet of raven-haired young women wearing little else—can that be Izz among them? A phalanx of willowy young men have donned dinner jackets and strung diamond chokers around their cygnine necks. Last off the elevators are a dozen downcast Gummis in shackles, prodded forward by two rows of very fit young men and women—Briony recognizes the pale-haired Scandinavian woman who leads them as the ship golf pro—each carrying with great bravado a shiny black Micro-Uzi, last seen in the hair-trigger hands of their captive Gummis.

Out of this resplendent throng steps Anna May Wang, nearly tripping over pleated palazzo pants so long they pool on the deck. She turns her weapon this way and that as if she would mow the passengers down with no regret.

"Esmiss Esmoor!" she yells out, "Esmiss Esmoor, you help us now!"

Mrs. Moore, wresting the bullhorn from Mimi's hands, leaves Briony's side and makes her way among the sunbeds, oversized beach toys, and drifts of discarded towels.

As she reaches Anna May, the workers in their motley outfits mob round them, hugging and kissing Mrs. Moore, some removing their jewels to festoon her coiled white hair and tunic, but she soon waves them away. Her face stern and her body rigid, she looks to Briony ill-suited for such adulation and bonhomie. She whispers into Anna May's ear, and Anna May, exhibiting uncertain mastery of her weapon, fires starboard and primarily out to sea, to the passengers' screams. The weapon's staccato report leaves serrated silence in its wake.

"Thank you, my dears! Thank you, Anna May!" She embraces her comrade and together they disentangle her new jewels from the pompoms on Anna May's fuchsia bolero.

Mrs. Moore lifts the bullhorn and turns to address the passengers as Mimi looks on, agog. "If I may introduce my fellow voyagers to Anna May Wang, leader of the *Emerald Tranquility* mutiny. I am merely the mutiny's spokesperson, just as Mimi here is Captain Kartoffeln's. I should begin by saying my friends mean you no harm."

Anna May tugs at Mrs. Moore's tunic and stands on tiptoe to murmur in her ear.

Mrs. Moore begins again. "My friends have not yet decided whether they mean you harm or not. Emotions, as you may well imagine, are running high. Having never participated in a mutiny before, they feel it may take some time to work out all the small details that combine to create a successful revolution."

"But what are their plans?" Roper James "Sav" Farquharson of the Australian fewmet-processing clan shouts out.

Mrs. Moore smiles as broadly as her natural reserve allows. "We have already achieved our primary goal."

"What's that then?" he shoots back.

"Why, inverting the power structure of the *Emerald Tranquility*. The last have become first and the first last. That's a start."

"What the hell does that even mean?" asks an elegant blonde, white towel draped like a cowl over her blistering shoulders.

"Matthew 20:16," Madame Rehbinder says calmly.

Mimi sounds fierce, even without the bullhorn. "And what will you do now you've achieved your so-called goal?"

"The very next thing we do" — Mrs. Moore points a commanding finger in her direction — "is march you off to the brig."

A murmur of consternation from among the passengers, but not much more than that. It strikes Briony that, in their eyes, Mimi's one of the help too.

"My little joke," Mrs. Moore says. "For now, no one's going to the brig. We will carry on as before, except from here on you will all have to do your own chores, your own cleaning up."

Old Major Chelmsworth Cholmondeley goes pale, his

cane clatters to the deck. Madame Rehbinder bends to retrieve it but her back's not up to it. She pats his palsied hand.

"As you can imagine," Mrs. Moore goes on, "putting a ship of this size out of commission may prove far easier than setting it to rights again. To be frank, we hadn't imagined we'd be this successful, so none of us have given much thought to repairing the engines or getting the toilets up and running again, as it were."

Anna May steps forward to speak in Mrs. Moore's ear once more.

Mrs. Moore beams. "That *is* good news — well done! Anna May informs me the ship engineers have come over to our side, not that it took much persuasion — have you any idea how little these men are paid? — and auxiliary power has already been restored to forty percent of the ship. Furthermore, the maids have agreed to supervise the cleaning of the staterooms and corridors, and to provide implements necessary for doing so. They will not, however, actually pitch in to help."

"Did we miss anything?" Briony starts as Teenah steps out onto Lido Deck, dazzling in a topaz-studded bandolier over an abbreviated maid's uniform. Kurd follows close behind, wearing a silver-lamé boiler suit and carrying a push broom nearly as long-spined as he.

Pumping her small fist, Teenah cries out, *"Venceremos!"*

Kurd pumps his skeletal fist too: *"Campesinos!"*

13

THE COMFORTING BREEZES OF the *Emerald Tranquility* at full sail no longer available, the ship has turned into a vast floating oven. Electricity comes and goes, along with aircon. In un-cooled corridors the 50-metre stroll to Kurd's penthouse suite becomes a death march. Mrs. Moore comes along reluctantly, murmuring about tasks left undone and deadlines unmet, but the promise of champagne — "I will allow myself one glass" — proves irresistible even to her.

"Such an unexpected honour to meet you at last, Mrs. Moore," Kurd says.

"I can't believe you organized the whole mutiny single-handed," Teenah exclaims. "What a feat!"

Briony watches as Mrs. Moore's eyes travel the minimalist splendour of Kurd's suite. "Am I to take it you are both *for* the mutiny?"

"But of course," Kurd says. "How could we not be?"

"We were for it even before it properly started," Teenah adds. "Our maid, Evangelina — she's really become like family — hinted something was up."

"Evangelista?"

"Isn't that what I just said?"

Mrs. Moore looks even more adamant than usual. "You clearly said 'Evangelina.'"

Kurd intervenes. "The important thing is Evangelista knows she can count on our full support."

Every austere surface of Kurd's suite glows — if the air smells of anything at all, it's of the lightest spritz of lemongrass.

"How have you kept it all so spotless?" Briony asks.

"Ah, my lovely Briony, you forget how we architects are so very OCD. There's so little to do on board now — it's a most fervent pleasure to pitch in, while Evangelista's preoccupied with more, shall we say, class-driven activities. She brought me a lovely basket of cleaning supplies and showed me how the industrial vacuum cleaner — a most impressive machine! — can be found in the cupboard just along the corridor. You must see what a tireless disinfector our Teenah has become. Darling, show them your matte-black respirator mask, so chic, and the special gloves that keep your delicate hands from growing claw-like because of the chemicals, like poor Evangelista's."

Teenah blushes. "Mrs. Moore and Briony don't want to see that, Kurd." She turns to Mrs. Moore. "Do you know I've only just discovered that stainless steel bathroom and kitchen fixtures shine most brightly when scoured with a toothbrush and a cup of baking soda mixed with a solution of three-percent hydrogen peroxide?"

"I am so heartened to see the two of you approaching all this in the proper spirit," Mrs. Moore says levelly.

"Let me top up your glass, Mrs. Moore." Teenah wields the Rehoboam with grace.

"Just a drop, dear."

"But you are both young," Briony points out. "What

about the older passengers—I mean, that's pretty much everyone—toiling in this heat, in the stifling corridors and on deck? Do you think Doña Cuantos Cuantos-Besos will be able to pilot a huge vacuum cleaner? Can you imagine Mr. Beauchamp De Groot, on the far side of ninety, down on his knees with a scrub brush and a cup of cleaning solvent?"

"I can imagine it very well," Mrs. Moore says.

"The thought of forcing old people to do menial labour in such conditions turns my stomach," Briony says.

"And how was your stomach," Mrs. Moore asks, "when you watched fathers, mothers, and children, grandmothers and grandfathers labouring in the stifling heat at the silk factory in Modigliano?"

"We missed that excursion." Teenah glances at Kurd. "But so terrible!"

Briony recalls how, from their glassy vantage point at the *Palacio de Patos Blancos* before the quake, the white-garbed workers at their looms looked so *picturesque* in the shimmering afternoon heat, as if they were a spectacle expressly staged for the passengers' amusement. "But because those people suffered and died, is it right that our own fellow travellers should suffer and die too?"

Kurd jumps in. "But of course not, Briony—no one's arguing—"

Mrs. Moore interrupts. "Your friend's right—no one would ever argue that. Nonetheless, in times of great change there may occur unforeseen and unavoidable collateral damage. I will spare you Robespierre's dictum about eggs and omelettes, but when you consider the history of our species and the untold horrors the rich have visited on the poor for so many thousands of years, of what import is an aged banker collapsing from overwork or heat prostration? Do you not think this happens every day — every minute! — to a poor person somewhere on this earth? How much can one rich person's torment weigh on the gargantuan scales of human suffering?"

And what is the point of responding, Briony thinks, when Mrs. Moore already possesses all the answers? Yet she tries. "Isn't it dangerous to say one life is worth more or less than another?"

"History incessantly reminds us the lives of the poor and the oppressed have less value than ours. They are disposable and figure in our headlines only when they perish in great numbers. The rich must suffer now because they deserve to, because it's their turn."

"A pretty heartless argument."

Mrs. Moore reaches out to touch her cheek. "Ah, always the sentimentalist — will you shed tears now over the hypothetical death of an arbitrageur?"

Briony feels a sudden urge to slap Mrs. Moore hard and knock the superciliousness right out of her. The more she speaks, the taller she grows — and the more her eyes flash with excitement. It strikes Briony that this is when she truly becomes hot and bothered, when her breathing goes shallow and her pulse dances, when passion rises and she gives herself up entirely. This is the wildest ecstasy for her: complete devotion to a cause. Not to me, Briony thinks, or to any other singular one, but to all those she's determined to defend and avenge.

"Have any of you seen that old surrealist film *The Discreet Charm of the Bourgeoisie?*" Mrs. Moore asks. "Directed by the great Luis Buñuel?"

Kurd and Teenah return Briony's blank stare.

"Oh," Briony finally says, "isn't he the one who made that short with the razor slicing through the woman's eyeball?"

Mrs. Moore nods enthusiastically. "In *The Discreet Charm,* six French bourgeois attempt to dine. Except they're constantly interrupted. At the first restaurant, the manager lies dead in an adjoining room, loudly mourned by his staff. At a subsequent dinner party, a curtain rises and the diners find themselves onstage in front of a full theatre, none of them knowing their lines. I believe terrorists gun them down at table at some point. Whatever the interruption though, in the next scene the six are alive once more, strolling down a country road, as avid for pleasure as ever, looking for another place to dine."

She scans the tastefully voided suite once more and turns her blaze on Kurd. "And you, how is it you don't think of yourself as rich?"

He goes pale. "You must understand these are merely the trappings of my profession. Architects, as you know, are classless. In order to win commissions, I must appeal to the rich, even to a certain extent mimic their excessive behaviour. At heart, though, I remain just this poor boy from Düsseldorf."

Mrs. Moore's already lost interest. "What about you?" she says to Teenah, "You too must be terribly poor in your tailored maid's uniform and fine jewels."

Tears form in Teenah's eyes. "Yes, I am poor too. I have only recently been disinherited."

"Such subversive zeal all around me." Mrs. Moore turns back to Briony. "And you, my dear, don't tell me you're poverty-stricken as well? You with your lavish penthouse, couture garments, and boarding-school manners?"

How can she defend herself without sounding as hollow and craven as Teenah and Kurd? "The manners I can't help, Mrs. Moore, and the fancy clothes are perks of my job."

The older woman looks startled. "*You* have a *job?*"

Briony explains about *Euphoria!* and her new-found homelessness.

"Imagine that." Mrs. Moore sighs. "I knew there was something off about you from the moment we met, but I would never have guessed your penury. You play your rich part to perfection. This leaves me in no doubt of where your sympathies lie."

It's not Mrs. Moore's easy judgement that hurts but rather the accuracy of her perception. Briony stands defenseless.

Mrs. Moore raises her glass. "Thank you so much, Briony, for the pleasure of meeting your delightful friends. You must be very happy to have their love and support and steadfast devotion to the cause."

"Mrs. Moore, *please.*"

The old woman smashes her flute on the ebony intarsia floor and is out the door before they can grasp what has happened.

"Wow!" Teenah says to the closed door.

"So fierce!" Kurd exclaims. Zealous tears roll down their faces. Only Briony is left high and dry.

IN THE PASSAGEWAY BETWEEN Kurd's penthouse and her own, Briony comes upon Viscount and Viscountess Grimsley-Arserton rolling along big orange rubber buckets. The Viscount's bucket is full to the brim with fresh — that is to say, foul — excrement; the Viscountess's vessel sloshes urine on the already-stained carpet.

Briony greets them both and asks if she may lend a hand.

"Most kind," the Viscount assures her, "but there's really no need."

"No worse than pitching in to help around the estate," the Viscountess adds, shooing a largish fly away from her aquiline nose. "Steady on, Bungo," she urges as the Viscount's bucket bounces off a baseboard.

Opening the door to her own suite, Briony discovers they've done a beautiful job — all surfaces immaculate and only the slightest after-odour, even in the ensuite.

Her first inclination upon leaving Kurd and Teenah was to rush down to Mrs. Moore's stateroom and — well, actually, her first urge in any fraught situation is to rush to her side.

The more circumspect and rageful Briony thinks, Fuck her and her heartless revolutionary bromides.

She uses the remote to illuminate and fill the sarcophagus bath and then strews pomelo-pomegranate bath salts over the churning water. As she's struggling out of Mrs.

Moore's linen tunic, she hears pounding at the door.

Rather than put the tunic back on — she doesn't want to be touched by anything that has touched *her* right now — she throws on her dressing gown and wrenches open the door.

Mimi.

She barges in. "Have you seen him?"

"Who?"

"Little Buddha."

"Not since this afternoon on Lido Deck."

"Wasn't that a disaster? I still can't get over the sight of those maids and butlers all dolled up and waving guns in our faces."

"Not actually in our faces, Mimi. They were jubilant but restrained, I thought."

Mimi gives her a hard look. "Since when are you infused with revolutionary spirit?"

She can't help laughing. "You may well ask."

"You're sure you haven't seen him? I was hoping he might have come to you."

"Have you checked the Sea-Breeze Non-Denominational Chapel?"

"I'm pretty sure I know where he is: Truffle Butter, the crew's lower-deck disco. The crew — the *workers* — are celebrating their victory there. They asked him to bless their *thé dansant*."

"Why don't you go down and find him?"

"They won't let me in — workers only."

"Little Buddha's not a worker. He's a monk."

"You actually fell for that?"

"What?"

"Honey, Little Buddha's not even Buddhist, let alone a monk. He's a grifter." Mimi laughs indulgently, "He plays his part, just like you and me."

"I see."

She shakes her head sadly, "And he hasn't returned."

"Maybe he decided to join in the celebrations?"

"He took his acolytes along."

"The golden boys with their credit-card machines? I haven't seen them in days."

"Mostly they hang out playing Go in their cabin — can you imagine, a dozen of them crammed into some below-deck rabbit hutch? — but Little B decided they were essential for the Truffle Butter blessing."

"They must have made quite a spectacle."

"Briony, you don't know how he gets when they've all had a few mai tais."

"How do you mean?"

"You're a big girl — I surely don't need to spell it out for you?"

"Possibly not."

Briony finds herself wishing she too were at Truffle Butter Disco, celebrating with golden abandon.

NEVER A GOOD IDEA, Briony tells herself, to drink yourself silly and pound on someone's door at 4 a.m., but here she is, pounding on Mrs. Moore's door at 4 a.m.

Warm hands cover her eyes. She spins round.

"Hello, Briony dear."

All fancied up, isn't she? Amethyst grapes glitter in her hair. Judging from her vinous breath, Briony grasps she's not the only silly drunk in front of the door.

"Been down the disco," Mrs. Moore says.

"Have you?"

"Don't give me that."

"Not giving you anything."

Mrs. Moore unlocks the door, draws Briony inside.

"You are hauteur writ large," the older woman says.

"Am I?"

"Just because I found your friends a bit—"

"Pretentious? Vulgar? Sycophantic?"

Mrs. Moore cocks her head. "You noticed?"

"How could I not? They're my friends. Well, Teenah is. Was. My friend."

"A bit more than that, no? I saw how she looked at you."

Mrs. Moore, jealous? "That's long over."

"Not for her, I'd say. And even *I* can see the appeal of him."

"You can?"

"The *length* of the man!"

How very un-Mrs. Moore–like, Briony thinks, I must get her drunk more often.

"A trifle dim though, don't you think? But both lovely, in their way." Mrs. Moore's eyes are very close to Briony's. "Have you had him as well?"

"Mrs. Moore!"

"And why wouldn't you? Skin like that, lips like those. *Youth.*"

"Oh, stop."

Mrs. Moore holds up her right arm so the ruched flesh sags, the fine down on her wrist gleams silvery white. "This is what I can offer when you come to me. Why bother coming at all when you could do so much better?"

"I wouldn't have said it was a rational process, my ending up here tonight with you."

"Fancy that!" Her nose darts forward to smell Briony's lips. "Had a wee nip, have we?"

She's in Briony's mouth in a way she's never been before, a stretch of hot, sinuous tongue. When it withdraws and she can breathe properly again, Briony finds she wants it back at once. If it stays out too long, more words will emerge from both their mouths, and honestly, what's the point?

She can accuse Mrs. Moore of self-righteousness, of having the body temperature of a salamander, of endless self-regard and pitiless indifference, of smug superiority. And she's sure Mrs. Moore has an equally long list of terms of opprobrium for her. But to what end? Briony knows who she is and knows as well that when they're together, she can't keep any of that in focus. Not when the heat's full on.

Who'd have thought an old woman could be so tough? All spit and gristle, she flattens Briony against the Farrow & Ball accent wall, bites her lower lip until Briony's saliva takes a carnivorous turn. Mrs. Moore tastes it too, pulls back.

"They — they've found him, you know."

"Who?"

"'Whom.'"

"Go fuck—"

"The captain.

"Where?"

"Meat freezer, crew's kitchen."

"Dead?"

"What do you think?'"

She climbs her way back to sobriety. "Who put him there, Mrs. Moore?"

"The chief officer. I gather Captain Kartoffeln was rough on his immediate subordinates."

"The chief officer locked him in to freeze to death?"

"It was completely innocent, I swear to you." She leans forth to lick the beads of sweat from Briony's brow until she pulls away with a start.

"How innocent can it be? He stuffed the captain in the freezer and the poor guy died. Very slowly."

"He was alive when the first officer hid him there in order to conceal his own participation in the mutiny. Some of his reactionary colleagues were conducting a full lower-decks search for the captain. Power was off at the time, so he naturally thought, 'I will stow the captain here for safekeeping and come back for him later.'"

"But he didn't."

"He couldn't—communications snafu. You know how these things can go, even with the best of intentions. Anna May and her cohorts, not realizing the first officer had joined their cause, arrested him. He couldn't make them understand the urgency of releasing the captain. When the power came back on, the first officer was already confined to brig."

Briony knows Mrs. Moore would draw her to her now, but she is made of lead.

"But we mustn't focus on this," Mrs. Moore says.

"What must we focus on instead of the captain's death?"

"Not the accidents or miscommunications or imbroglios — these are inevitable by-products of a sudden shift in the balance of power — but rather on the fact that, even in a partially armed rebellion, there have been so few casualties. My comrades have been most punctilious about this. It could have happened to anyone."

"But it happened to the captain."

"I was speaking of the first officer. What he did was not volitional."

"That's a *huge* relief. 'So few casualties'? *So few?*" Briony hadn't meant to shout. Now it's her turn to shove Mrs. Moore across the room. "How many?"

"You are asking for an exact tally?"

"Yes. Including elderly passengers who have worked themselves to death in the blazing sun."

"They *died* — they were not killed."

"How many?"

"Fourteen."

"Fourteen!"

"The captain, three crew, and ten passengers."

"Ten!"

"But only the very oldest, feeblest ones, who would have gone soon in any case. With the possible exception of Doña Cuantos Cuantos-Besos. That, I will be the first to admit, ought not to have happened."

"What? What happened?"

"She was vacuuming the wide central corridor on Maybach Deck, and doing quite a credible job of it, I understand, for a woman used to being waited on hand and foot. Around the corner came Viscount and Viscountess Grimsley-Arserton pushing their slop buckets. They collided head-on with Doña Cuantos Cuantos-Besos. The bucket — the one containing urine, I assume — tipped over, and the poor woman was electrocuted. What with one thing and another, the maintenance staff haven't been able to properly inspect and service the vacuum cleaners lately."

"But that's horrible!"

"We will get them back on a proper rota very soon, I'm sure."

"Horrible that Doña Cuantos Cuantos-Besos had to die!"

"Yes, yes, of course. It *is* horrible. Because we know her, because you know her — I never met the woman. She is, she was real, while the nameless millions who die each year because of war, exploitation, environmental desecration, systemic racism — they fail to touch you at all. They are only statistics. Their sacrifice has been necessary to maintain Western democracy and prosperity. Perhaps all this will be easier for you to bear if you think of Doña Cuantos Cuantos-Besos as a statistic: an exceptionally rich woman who met her end in the pointless way numberless poor people do every hour of every day."

"This is just so much sophistry."

"'Sophistry'?" Mrs. Moore looks at her quizzically. "Not a word I would expect from you."

"I learned one or two things while idling my way through McGill."

"You went to McGill? That is a very good school."

"You're just like the rest of them."

"Rest of whom?"

"The rich you despise so much. Impressed by a smug, mediocre institution because of its name."

"I fail to see how you can dismiss an entire university simply because you didn't like it there."

"How can you dismiss an entire class of people because you hate them?"

"I don't hate them."

"No?"

"You must understand this is strictly impersonal. I hate what they've done, what they continue to do. What about you, Briony? You've spent much of your life promoting the rich. You've catered to them, pampered them, emulated them — look how you dress and speak! — in your fraudulent, aspirational way."

"Thank you so much for summarizing my empty, pointless life with such precision."

"After you've served them so faithfully — so servilely — what have the rich ever done for you?"

She's got me there, Briony says to herself. "Not one fucking thing, but I have to make a living somehow."

Mrs. Moore scoffs. "You and that glossy rag you work for promote being rich as the ultimate value, the summit we'd all like to reach, and if we can't manage that, at least we get to delight in the brilliance of those who did attain it or were born there. We elevate them with our quenchless dreams of longing.

"Deep down we know we'll never succeed in joining

them, but how pleasing, how comforting, to ogle them from a distance, to laugh at their foibles and giggle at their extravagances and heartlessness. As we recognize that we can never be them, we come to see ourselves as failures and thus fully inhabit our own shame, our essential worthlessness. We're losers and we deserve to be. Looking at the rich, we accept our inalterable position in the grander scheme of things, and thus perpetuate a system that makes us feel small and inadequate."

Briony knows everything she says is true, this mirror Mrs. Moore holds up to her own imitation of life. But the solutions she offers! "You think we should exterminate them all?"

"Briony, Briony." She extends her arms as though she would take her into them. "When have I ever said that? Even if I had, how would I, an old woman with no wealth to speak of, with no power, ever be capable of such an undertaking? Ha! Bad pun. Don't you see that in my heart of hearts I know the situation to be irreversible, the cause lost before we've fairly begun? Whatever victories we attain on this ship will be, first and foremost, pyrrhic."

"Then what in hell do you think you're doing?"

"It is a gesture that must be made."

"As a kind of warning?"

She shakes her head. "Not even that. More like a momentary unsettling of the world as I know it. An emblem, if you will."

"You're deliberately misleading your followers for the sake of some ludicrous symbolic action?"

"Briony, I'm comforting the afflicted and afflicting the

comfortable — as a journalist, you must know this maxim. For simplicity's sake, let's say I'm presenting the rich with a *memento mori* and be done with it."

"Once you've reminded them of their own mortality and shamelessness, what then?"

Mrs. Moore laughs. "I don't ask for much, only something that creates a sense of unease, a niggling moment of insecurity, a presentiment for the rich that one day they too may suffer as they sail along on their own high-end Raft of the Medusa."

"That would satisfy you?"

Mrs. Moore reaches out to touch Briony's inflamed cheek. "Darling, I'm just like you — I'll never be satisfied. This is what capitalism's done to us all. But at least we're making a start. At least we're doing something critical, no matter how insignificant it may seem."

"I hope you're not including me in that 'we.' You can stamp out all the revolutionary boilerplate you want, and people who have no hope may follow. But don't implicate me in the death and destruction you've unleashed."

Mrs. Moore stares at Briony. "Then what on earth are you doing here with me?"

"You know the answer to that."

"You may hide behind cloying emotion all you want, but really, you are just like me — hopeless."

Briony's mouth falls open. Oh, *touché*, you gnarly bitch.

14

WAY TOO MUCH GOLD going on here, in Briony's opinion. Draped in gold lamé, all of Little Buddha's minions hold gold triangles in one hand, small gold beaters in the other. Little Buddha sits at their centre, Mimi at his side, both cocooned in cascades of gold muslin.

The corpses fan out before them, all encased in gold-brocade tablecloths permanently borrowed from the Sea-Change Lounge: Captain Kartoffeln; Doña Cuantos Cuantos-Besos; Madame Rehbinder (a heat stroke followed by an actual stroke as she polished the starboard rails on Cabriolet Deck); little, unfortunate Cecily Tybor, discovered that morning in a lifeboat (don't ask); a number of other passengers (such a gusty day!) whose names Briony didn't get; three crew members, all from the engine room (poor Viktor).

Mrs. Moore is nowhere in evidence: "Rituals, empty words, and the meretricious comfort of organized religion — what do I want with that?"

Mimi picks up her own gold mallet and with shaking hand strikes a golden gong three times.

"The thirty-five names of the Buddhas of Confession I will now recite," Little Buddha says.

"Oh, Little B — all thirty-five?"

He proceeds unheeding: *"Sakyamuni!"*

The minions strike their triangles and open their small mouths: "We could die!"

"*Vajraparmardi!*" Little Buddha shouts against the wind.

The golden boys sing out: "We can't die!"

"*Ratnarsis!*" Little Buddha's voice cracks, whether from sorrow or a dirty hangover, who can say?

The golden boys give it their adolescent all: "What if we die?"

"*Nagesvararaja!*"

"We could die!"

"*Virasena!*"

"We can't die!"

"*Ratnagni!*"

"What if we die?"

Looking around her, Briony notices the sunbeds are less thronged today. The passengers that have made it hold once-white towels above their heads for shade. Revolting crew members are much more numerous, though they're a shadowy presence, lounging beneath the canvas awnings, their extravagant finery muted by the black armbands they wear to honour their fallen comrades.

Only Anna May Wang stands throughout the service, her jewels refracting the unbearable sunlight, the ostrich plume on her cloche drooping in the humid breeze.

"*Ratnacandraprabha!*"

"We could die!"

"*Amoghadarsi!*"

"We can't die!"

"Ratnacandra!"

"What if we die?"

Mimi hits the gong so hard the head of her mallet flies off and plummets into the swimming pool. She shouts at Little Buddha: "That's enough names! More than enough." She lowers her voice. "We've got to move this thing along or we'll have even more bodies to dispose of."

Refrigerated till now in the morgue and various kitchen meat-lockers, the cadavers have ripened beneath their brocade. Briony feels the rising odour alone provides reason enough for haste.

The morgue workers, resplendent in purloined silk kimonos, wheel the captain's gurney toward the railing. At Little Buddha's signal, the golden boys surround the gurney and sing in high voices.

"Hallelujah." Inevitably. Fucking Leonard Cohen. Countryman or not, he has a lot of answer for, unleashing that sepulchral dirge on an unsuspecting world. She feels she will throw herself over the side too if she must listen to it one second longer.

The golden boys have joined hands and sway gently back and forth to the slow monotony of the hymn.

On about the forty-second "Hallelujah," she can hold herself back no longer. The heat, the putrefaction, the lugubrious melody — she rushes to the rail and vomits the contents of the lunch Luis scrounged for her — shrimp cocktail with lukewarm Marie Rose sauce — over the side.

"Hey, you who are up there — stop this obediently."

The bearded man now rappelling from balcony to balcony up the blazing side of the *Emerald Tranquility* alongside so many other near-naked, bearded men has a familiar voice, but it's the Balmain "B" on his bathing slip that gives him away.

"Gigot!"

"Ma chère!" He nearly loses his grip on the nylon cord clutched in his sun-darkened hands.

"Be careful," she calls down. "What on earth are you doing? Are these your friends?"

He grins. A missing upper left canine gives him a raffish look. "Can't you guess? We are *les pirates*, come to overtake you." He calls out to the other rappelling men. "Is this not right, *mes pôtes?*"

The other men let out a lusty cheer. *"Vive les pirates!"*

"Why are they speaking French, Gigot?" Briony yells.

"Many of them are escaped political prisoners from Les Îles de la Société."

"The Society Islands?" Briony wonders if such a place exists. "Why do you want to take us over?"

Only two balconies below her now, he's growing short of breath. "We mean you no 'arm."

"No 'arm!" the chunky, bearded climber to his left yells, and the others take it up: "No 'arm! No 'arm!"

"We want merely the ship," Gigot explains.

"The ship's in pretty bad shape. Many people have already died."

His right hand joins his left one on the rail — his nails are a mess, she notices. He leaps onto Lido Deck along with a number of his piratical cohort.

Little Buddha, the golden boys, and the morgue workers step away from the captain's gurney in alarm. It trundles to the rail, and the gold cloth containing his earthly remains plunges into the sea.

Cries of *"Attention!"* and *"Zut alors!"* rise angrily from the pirates still rappelling.

Gigot surveys the remaining gurneys, the telltale shapes beneath the napery. "But we disturb the funeral rites. Our profound *condoléances!*" He and his men take in the wasted passengers reclining on sunbeds and the gaudy mutineers beneath white awnings. "So sorry!" Gigot cries, and the men echo him: *"Désolé!"*

The mutineers emerge from the shadows, silk and jewels coruscating in the sun, Micro-Uzis prominently displayed. Gigot's men, scores and scores of them on deck now, line up behind the gurneys. Each holds a Beretta machine gun, which to Briony's mind is the most elegant and compact of all semi-automatic weapons — she did a feature for *Euphoria!* once called "Small Arms and the Man" — capable of squeezing off a single accurate bullet or spraying magazine after magazine of them.

"Hands up! Hands up!" It occurs to Briony that Anna May sounds like a crazed '80s disco singer.

The sun-dazed passengers on the sunbeds slowly raise their hands.

"Not you!" Anna May scolds the oldies. *"Piratas!"*

Little Buddha steps forward: "We must in harmony come together to better — "

A single report from either a Micro-Uzi or a Beretta splits the air. Little Buddha collapses in a heap of muslin.

A golden minion cries out and also falls to the ground. His companions crowd round him. Little Buddha rights himself and parts the minions to inspect the wincing golden boy. "Flesh wound only," he announces. "He will most surely survive." He lowers his voice: "Mimi, you perhaps have a clean handkerchief?"

Mimi appears to have zoned out entirely. A bearded pirate sporting a single chandelier earring aims his Beretta at Mimi's head. Poor Mimi, Briony thinks, this must feel so *déjà vu*. "Guns down," he shouts at the mutineers, "or the lady she is *défunte*."

Perplexed murmuring among the mutineers.

Briony's mother always insisted bilingualism would advance her in the world one day. "Dead!" she cries out. "Lower your weapons or the lady is dead."

Some consultation as the mutineers wonder if the lady would be such a loss.

An enormous concussion knocks mutineers, pirates, and passengers sideways. Gigot catches Briony as she falls. No one thinks to catch Little Buddha: he rolls across Lido Deck, benignly smiling.

"We move! We move!" Anna May screams from a supine position. The ship, becalmed for so long, does move, but slowly, soundlessly, with no humming vibration of the ship's engines.

"Come quickly and regard!" Gigot urges, and everyone who can runs toward the bow. Two dilapidated tugboats — army-green paint jobs nearly obscured by rust and barnacles — pull the *Emerald Tranquility* forward, winches straining. Like baby ducks following their mothers, a flotilla of Zodiacs tethered to the tugs bob along in their wake. The name of the tugboat on the left in faded aluminum paint reads *The Sheepdog II*; the one on the right, *Muzukashii Desu*.

Gigot points at the Zodiacs. "This is how we arrive here, you see?"

Briony does see — the flat sea, the absence of land. "But where are you towing us?"

"Not far, my dear Briony. Not so very far."

"Yo, *mes pirates!*" Gigot shouts. "We come in peace, more or less. Drop down your guns, *s'il vous plaît*."

Amid cries of *"putain de merde"* and *"nique ta mère pédé,"* a handful of pirates lay their weapons on the deck. Briony recognizes "Fuck your mother, faggot," from French-immersion primary school, but she's always been unsure about *"putain de merde"* — does it mean "shitty slut" or "fucking shit"?

"Mais non!" Gigot gesticulates wildly. "Please not to place your guns *on* the deck. Pick them up but do not to shoot them. We have the guns, they have the guns, everybody die — *je vous en prie!*"

With a sharp nod of her head, Anna May indicates the mutineers must lower their weapons too. It's clear they're outnumbered. "We wait" — she pauses dramatically — "and see."

A Canadian standoff, Briony concludes.

The golden boys burst into applause as their wounded *confrère* struggles to stand — a small lace handkerchief flutters round his left biceps. Mimi lies prone and unmoving on a nearby sunbed.

Indicating the still-loaded gurneys, Little Buddha exhorts the crowd: "We still have before us a most sombre and unwelcome duty to fulfill. Boys!"

The minions join the morgue workers and together they push the gurneys to the railing. Briony turns away at the last moment but hears a volley of splats as the cadavers meet the sea.

Teenah and Kurd step out onto Lido Deck wearing matching jumpsuits in camo-print neoprene.

"Hello," Kurd says, "we are moving forward."

15

HOW STRANGE FOR BRIONY to find herself in her own bed in her odourless suite and glimpse — after the white-hot glare of the past few days — blue skies and white fluffy clouds beyond the French doors. When three mangy palm trees drift past, she hurries out onto the balcony.

If she were a less prepossessed person she might cry out "Land!" as the *Emerald Tranquility* nears a dismal stretch of shoreline. Abandoned vehicles of all sizes, scorched driftwood, coils of oily rope, and tangles of cast-off fishing nets litter the sand — all dwarfed by a curving sheet of corroded metal standing upright, like a misplaced Richard Serra.

"Briony, but you are up with the chicken!" Luis lays out breakfast china and silver. "It's all right if you eat out here in the fresh air?"

She wipes granulated sleep from her eyes. "Luis, what are you doing here?"

"Sorry?"

"Haven't you joined the mutineers?"

He looks stunned. "I am shock you think such a thing, Miss Briony."

"I didn't mean to offend you. I simply thought —"

"You thought I joined the *lumpenproles* like everybody else? Became part of these raggedy-ass rabble? I am a far better materialist than this. They are all but *falsos* in borrowed fancy clothes, with no proper analysis or class consciousness."

"'*Falsos*'? Fakes?"

"Maybe."

He places fresh fruit, brioches, various compotes, a generous cheese plate, and a goblet of guava juice on the table, and darts inside to return with a silver *cafétière*.

"Where did you get all this?"

"I take good care of my Briony, yes? All along I am sneaking foods from the kitchen and from the restaurants, the snacking bars, the *gelaterias*, and hiding them in your fridge, your cupboards.

"You came in here even when it smelled bad?"

"I'm a professional. When real revolution comes, I promise you I'll be ready and willful, but if you think for a single moment I'll join these *idiotas*, then I'm sorry to say you underestimate me."

She takes a sip of the guava juice. "This is ice-cold. How is this possible when there is no power?"

"I have my connections." His broad smile begs her to ask more.

"What connections?"

"You know this word 'homintern'?"

"Secret sissy society?"

"*Si!* There is always power for people who know where to look for it. You think the aircon in your bedroom comes out of my brown ass?"

She realizes she hadn't even noticed the air conditioning, ever assuming creature comforts come to her automatically because they always have, because she deserves them.

"You really shouldn't dismiss the mutineers. They too are professionals, or at least skilled workers. Maybe not as high as butlers on the crew hierarchy, but surely part of a true working class. They too have been schooled in —" she's about to say "Marxist dialectics" when he interrupts.

"They are so naive they need this old white lady to organize their rebellion. How they have been schooled? *How?*" He pours her coffee with such indignation the cup overbrims. "They are so full of false consciousness they are ignorant even of the difference between 'use-value' and 'exchange-value.'"

"I happen to know" — Briony's dismayed by her own haughty tone — "many of the crew have been reading up on the meaning of revolution and, er, theory, and *praxis,* and so on."

"You think maybe I don't know this? Your friend, this tall old lady, every cruise she comes and invites young girls into her room. She's not a true revolutionary at all, only an optimistic lesbo."

"'Opportunistic'?"

"That too."

Why is she so offended on Mrs. Moore's behalf when he speaks the truth? "I don't think she's opportunistic, Luis."

"Because you fancy her," he says with a pout.

"She's not allowed in your little all-boy homintern because she's a 'lesbo'? How's that for false consciousness? Where's your solidarity with your intersectional comrades?"

"I know what I am and am proud of my sexual stripe, but why do I have to let a rich old lady in too?"

"Because she's..."

"What about you, Briony? Where do you stand?"

"Unlike you and Mrs. Moore with your complete certitude, I've never known where I stand."

"I see." She can see he's close to laughing at her vehemence while still being furious with her.

"And I'm fine with that, you little *maricón*."

He starts to giggle. "My Briony, I've never seen you so flaming. Like this different woman."

She's giggling too. "'Fiery'?"

He nods.

"Mrs. Moore is — Mrs. Moore is —"

"Mrs. Moore is a tall old white lesbo — she eats you up!"

"'Out,' Luis — she eats me out."

She can see him committing this new phrase to memory. "All right, all right, since she's your girlfriend she's an okay old lady."

"That's better."

"For a lesbo." He sidesteps the brioche she launches at him.

SHE FINDS MRS. MOORE holding forth onstage in the Broadway Melody Theatre, white tunic aglow against the scarlet curtain. Crew members in withered fancy dress lounge in the curving rows of seats, along with an unexpected number of *les pirates,* still sporting their black leather bandoliers. It's stifling, even with the theatre doors wide open. Mrs. Moore doesn't appear to notice.

"Once there was honour in labour, once there were unions to protect workers and fight for their bargaining power. But in late capitalism the most important commodities have become ethereal — ones and zeroes, data, apps. Workers kept poor by corporate states are no longer even a class. They have become the ultimate ideal commodity: faceless, powerless, biddable, convenient, transportable, expendable, disposable. We have fast food deprived of all nutritional value, fast fashion falling apart as you wear it, and now the cheap and docile fast workers, overburdened and underpaid, numerous beyond belief and still multiplying even as they live on the furthest margins of survivability.

"As the middle class see their own jobs and power evaporate and they too tumble down to worker level, soon all that will be left is a narrow class of wealthy technocrats, needed to keep AI and automatons up and running, the same automatons that will take from you whatever pitiable jobs you've eked out of a dying system."

One of the pirates tries to get a chant of *"Solidarité"* going, but under Mrs. Moore's baleful gaze it quickly peters out.

"What we're seeing is the collapse of the concept of social and economic classes altogether, with one great undifferentiated mass condemned to a global hell of deprivation, disease, and rapidly diminishing life expectancy, while an infinitesimal number of the hyper-privileged live in unimaginable, self-perpetuating luxury.

"Our only hope rests in the fact that there are so few of them and so many of us. I cannot promise anything will come from this gaping disparity, but it does give us a glimmer of hope."

Mrs. Moore pauses, and her audience bursts into a cacophony of languages.

Anna May Wang steps onstage and relieves Mrs. Moore of her headset. "Now we have spontaneous translators, please."

"Simultaneous," Mrs. Moore corrects.

Briony thinks this should have occurred as Mrs. Moore spoke — isn't that what "simultaneous" means? But no — a dozen people hurry onstage and begin translating all at once — into Spanish and French, Arabic and Polish, Mandarin and possibly Latvian, Hindi, Tagalog, and Farsi.

Mrs. Moore steps down from the stage and makes her way toward Briony.

"I didn't expect to see you here."

Briony offers her hand to shake.

Mrs. Moore looks down at it. "It's come to this?" She leans in to kiss Briony's cheek. Eyes lashes lips breath skin scent small-raised-mole-above-her-left-eye — altogether a wrenching tsunami.

Briony steps back. "They say we'll be there soon."

"They?"

"Gigot."

"And where is there?"

"Gigot calls it Yomia."

"This I must see."

Briony follows Mrs. Moore out of the theatre and along

the starboard passageway, where a handful of passengers have congregated at the rail: Viscount and Viscountess Grimsley-Arserton, minus their slop buckets; Count Guido Malodoroso, in stained singlet and burgundy pyjama bottoms; a badly sunburned Mrs. Spitz-Basenji, white plastic toilet brush in one hand, frowsy Pomeranian — Mrs. Miniver — in the other. The biggest shock is old Major Chelmsworth Cholmondeley, propped up by his malacca cane and almost disappearing into the big white chef's apron he's wrapped twice round his ancient frame. What can he be doing in the kitchen? Briony wonders. The man's too weak to lift a pot lid. He must miss Madame Rehbinder terribly.

In the distance, a jagged skyline's nearly eclipsed by serpentine yellow clouds coiling round it. As they draw nearer, the strange shapes resolve into tall, malformed towers and windowless walls of grey or blue metal. At their centre, the great prow of a ship rises from the beach, the sand striated in ochre, liquid mercury, blue-black oil.

Closer still, the air itself changes colour, takes on texture and flavour, grit and sulphur, clogging Briony's nose and throat, stinging her eyes. Viscountess Grimsley-Arserton politely tries to suppress the creaking of her lungs. Her husband points at the water below them, which churns a vibrant orange with furtive streaks of turquoise and cadmium yellow.

As the tugboats manoeuvre the *Emerald Tranquility* parallel to the shore, small figures emerge from distant, phantasmagoric structures. First a handful, then dozens and dozens of men, women, and children pour out to greet them. Some of the men are dressed, like Gigot's pirates, in multicoloured briefs and little else, while many of the women wear saris, their colours faded and begrimed. But the majority of both men and women are haphazardly clad in strategically placed scraps of this and that—mouldy feathers, blanched palm fronds, plastic flowers, canvas scraps. Children run about naked except for turbans on the boys' heads, fashioned from white hand towels.

As they float closer still, the people begin serenading the great ship over the sound of crashing surf. The words are at first unintelligible to Briony, but snatches of meaning soon emerge, along with a recognizable melody.

Je renierais ma patrie
...mes amis
...n'importe quoi
Si tu me le demandais

"What are they singing?" Mrs. Spitz-Basenji asks Briony.

"It's an Édith Piaf song of unbridled masochism. She's telling her lover that she'll renounce her country, her friends, everything—if he asks her to."

Gigot joins Briony and the other passengers at the rail. "You see," he says to Briony and Mrs. Moore, "They sing us the welcome. It's so *émouvant*. Everyone must know this wonderful song of my old country and now the anthem of my new one."

The singers reach the opaque waves and stand swaying in the surf:

Si un jour, la vie t'arrache à moi
Si tu meurs, que tu sois loin de moi

Briony continues her own simultaneous translation: "If one day you're torn from me, if you die, if you're far from me." Gigot places his hand over his heart, eyes swimming with tears as he sings along:

Peu n'importe, si tu m'aimes
Car moi je mourrai aussi.

Hell of a national anthem, Briony thinks as she translates the last lines: "None of this matters, if you love me, because I will die too."

A single tear runs down Mrs. Spitz-Basenji's parbroiled cheek.

A tall, almost naked man emerges from the crowd, a big hibiscus bloom in his luxuriant sun-streaked hair, his body so brown, his muscles so articulated he looks like an intricately carved fetish object.

"Little Gigot!" the man shouts across the water.

"Frank!" Gigot calls back, "Frank Joy!"

"You bring us big booty," Frank Joy exults as he takes in the mammoth *Emerald Tranquility*.

"What we used to call a fine specimen of a man," Mrs. Moore murmurs to Briony.

"Whose side are you on?"

Mrs. Moore rolls her eyes. "Oh Briony, let an old woman dream."

"Is he not *magnifique*?" Gigot sighs.

16

DISEMBARKATION PROVES A TEDIOUS PROCESS. Yomia has no proper gangway, not even a pier, so everyone's taken ashore in Zodiacs, a process hindered by the ill-health of the passengers, many of whom must be transported lying down. The mutinous crew overload their Zodiacs, nearly overturning them, but clamber out safely onshore, laughing and cheering. Anna May Wang leads the way. Mrs. Moore and Briony come in the last boat with a misty eyed Gigot, who, minutes before they reach shore, leaps into the putrescent surf and slo-mo sprints toward Frank Joy. Briony watches as they greet each other with the passionate tropes lovers trot out after long absences. It's been all of two days.

Little Buddha struggles along the strand, his progress impeded by waterlogged muslin. "So," he says to Briony and Mrs. Moore, "to what brave new world have we come?"

"Where's Mimi?" Briony asks.

"She came ashore long ago with other passengers, for she is not feeling all tip-top. The kindly pirates have transported her to the island hospital. I immediately will proceed there and encourage her back to consciousness."

"I'm sure she'll be better soon," Mrs. Moore says, "now she's back on dry land."

Little Buddha wanders off, wrappings trailing in the mucky sand.

Gigot approaches, Frank Joy in hand. "I will please introduce you to my most valuable friend."

Briony finds it hard to look at Frank Joy — so much of him on display, including the graphic manifestation of his delight at reuniting with Gigot. For these same reasons, she finds it hard to look away.

"Welcome to our small island, ladies." Frank Joy flicks aside the curls cascading over his right eye. His accent's hard to place — definitely not French, but not quite English either, as if he once attended an American School in Beirut or Geneva.

Mrs. Moore ignores his proffered hand. "Are we here as your guests or your captives, Mr. Joy?"

"Captives?" Frank Joy laughs.

"Les belles captives, franchement," Gigot adds.

"You won't in any way be restrained or sequestered, for there's nowhere for you to escape to. Our boundaries are liquid, our nearest neighbours 1,000 kilometres away. You and your fellow passengers will be well treated, I dare say better cared for here than on the *Emerald Tranquility*, for many of them appear undernourished, dehydrated, or worse."

Briony starts to explain how this came to be, but Mrs. Moore gets there first. "You see, Mr. Joy, we have been conducting a small social experiment on our cruise, reversing the usual hierarchies that pertain to passengers and workers. We have found that —"

Frank Joy interrupts: "Gigot tells me you're the leader of the mutiny."

"Oh, 'leader,'" Mrs. Moore says, blushing, "I hardly think I was all that. I've been more of a catalyst than —"

He interrupts once more: "We too are conducting a social experiment here on Yomia. 'Utopia' has become such a dirty word I hesitate to apply it to our little endeavour, and 'intentional community' sounds so dry, don't you find?"

Gigot nods enthusiastically.

"We prefer to call it harmonious synergy, where people of all colours, castes, and creeds come together in comity to create —"

It's Mrs. Moore's turn to break in: "I thought you were common pirates."

Frank Joy winks at Gigot. "Our little joke. We do liberate ships, from cruise liners to oil tankers, and we often subsume passengers and crews into our synergy when they show themselves sympathetic to our cause."

"And if they're unsympathetic?"

Frank Joy beams at Mrs. Moore. "Eventually, don't you see, everyone's sympathetic."

"How convenient for you."

"But don't you find," he continues, "great social movements are like this? At first there's reluctance, even resistance, but with judicious management of social assumptions and realities, almost everyone falls in line, and for those who don't ex-societal roles are found."

It occurs to Briony he means death.

"And our crew," Mrs. Moore asks. "What will happen to them?"

Frank Joy tugs at his loincloth. "I can assure you we will take good care of them."

"That's what worries me."

He laughs as if Mrs. Moore has told a wonderful joke. "In any case, none of this actually applies to you and your friends, for we have entirely different plans for you."

"Do tell."

Briony finds the look on Mrs. Moore's face hard to read. Does she see this swaggering, gorgeous man, her junior by many decades, as her enemy or her distant twin? He's more than her equal at spinning words to create new and theoretically attractive possibilities for human conduct.

"Although we have commandeered smaller cruise ships before, we've never succeeded in capturing anything approaching the size of the *Emerald Tranquility*, nor a ship that has offered such an illustrious passenger list. I understand a number of the wealthiest have already been lost to shipboard mishaps, yet enough remain that we can offer them up to loved ones or corporate boards and ransom them for princely sums."

Gigot throws an arm over Frank Joy's sun-patinated shoulder. "Frank has the many plans for making Yomia a nicer place, with boulevards and schools for the little children and maybe fountains and a large *piscine*."

"But first," Frank Joy says, "you must see Yomia as it is, warts and all, and for that you'll have the best possible guide." He beams at Gigot. "I only wish I could accompany you. Unfortunately, my schedule doesn't permit. But we'll meet again later in the day, once Gigot has delivered you to your final resting place."

Final resting place, Briony thinks. In a utopia, paranoia's always appropriate.

"Adieu," Gigot calls after Frank Joy's retreating back, muscles shifting like blind moles beneath his sheeny skin.

Over his shoulder she watches as the pirates use the barrels of their weapons to gather the mutineers and the rest of the crew together and herd them away.

In the far distance, a smaller contingent of over-armed hearties lead a double line of shackled Gummis into the desolate scrubland beyond the beach.

WITH GIGOT AT THE WHEEL, they bounce along in an ancient U.S. Army jeep that time has stripped down to essentials: patched-over tires, wobbly steering column, seats loosely bolted to floorboards between which Briony glimpses racing sand.

Corroded prows and hulls from dismembered tankers and cruise ships thrust up from the earth, while propellers big as city buses and bow-fronted wheelhouses loll on their sides. Cross-sections of stacked ship staterooms eight or ten storeys tall stand upright on low dunes or on the shore itself, like tall white hotels with their façades ripped off, furniture and bathroom fixtures open to the air.

Barefoot workers descend like spelunkers on blackened ropes into the below-deck chambers where great engines once throbbed. Some carry tools — wrenches, hammers, rusty saws — but most work bare-handed as they render the lowering metal carcasses. Others haul away buckets overflowing with engine oil, or sway along with wreaths of copper wiring slung over emaciated shoulders.

Cubic bails of compressed metal form a wall between

the ship-breaking area and the town proper, which is low-slung and decrepit, shanties cobbled together from cardboard, corrugated steel, mosquito netting, clothespins. Gigot whisks them past a brief market with fly-raddled displays of blackened bananas and grey-skinned oranges side by side with rotting fish corpses that glow from within and a single deflated octopus.

"All free!" Gigot cries as he side-swipes a listing pallet of saffron rice bags. "No money in Yomia! Everything free."

As the packed-earth road begins to rise, the shantytown spreads out below them, beige and grey and overhung by darkening clouds.

"We leave now the lower city with its free houses for all workers," Gigot tells them.

Mrs. Moore whispers in Briony's ear: "If the workers labour for no money, since none exists, doesn't this make them slaves?"

Briony nods. Yomia's falling into place in a disheartening way. She shouts against the stiff wind: "Gigot, where are *our* workers?"

"Who?"

"The *Emerald Tranquility* crew. Where are they being taken?"

"No worries, Briony — they're being processed today."

"Processed?" A note of horror in Mrs. Moore's voice.

"Most of them go to the camp. For showers and *repas*."

"Camp?" Briony's turn to show alarm. *"Showers?"*

"Only 24 little hours," Gigot shouts, "before we finish their houses. Also, the hair grooming."

"There is a beauty salon in the camp?" Mrs. Moore asks.

Gigot laughs. "No, no. Grooming for *les puces*. They cut the hairs off so they're more easier to see."

"*Emerald Tranquility* workers don't have fleas," Briony says.

"No?" Gigot says. "Now they will never."

"You said *most* of the workers go to the camp," Mrs. Moore says. "What about the others?"

"Some run away," Gigot says. "No problem. We will captivate them soon."

"I see." Mrs. Moore taps his shoulder. "May we go there now?"

"Where?"

"The workers' camp."

Gigot's aghast. "*Mais non*, not today, please. Too many things for them to do. Tomorrow you'll review all ship workers in their new houses."

"And the passengers," Briony asks, "they're in this camp too?"

"Ah no, Briony." Gigot grins. "They are kept most well in the nice hospital. You'll see very soonish."

He shifts into first to propel them up a steep incline. As they round a wide curve, the sparse vegetation of the beach and town — mainly seaweed and leeched bracken — gives way to scrub forest and wiry grass. Climbing higher still, they encounter dense labyrinths of trees with blade-like leaves, white blossoms, and small globular fruit.

"What is this lovely tree?" Mrs. Moore asks Gigot.

"This is the pong pong tree, fruit like the little white balls. Very pretty."

"Beautiful."

"But never to eat," he admonishes. "It'll kill the old lady like you *tout de suite*. Stand under tree in rain, you die too."

"Goodness."

"Sometimes called suicide tree," Gigot says cheerfully. "Even the sweet smell of *les fleurs* will attack —"

"We get it, Gigot," Briony says.

"Very safe island though."

They jolt onto a wide paved road — the first they've encountered on Yomia — that bisects the long valley they're entering, with neat bamboo huts ranged along the green-fringed cliffs above them. Nodding toward them Gigot says, "For *les pirates*!" Semi-naked men walk the high paths snaking from hut to hut. "Very nice!"

Not a glimpse of the sea up here, or of ship-rendering, or the shantytown, and not even a trace of pollution. At the far end of the valley Gigot pulls up at a hammered-bronze gate set into a bamboo stockade. He honks the jeep's trumpeting horn and the gates scrape open. More multi-decked towers of cruise-ship staterooms bound the courtyard on three sides, their seaward walls replaced by louvred windows and rustic wooden balconies.

Onto one of the highest balconies emerge Teenah and Kurd, changed out of their workers' clothing: Teenah now in a python-skin mini dress, Kurd sporting suede lederhosen and a black organdy crop-top. "Briony! Mrs. Moore!" they yell down, "Welcome to Adrastus Palace."

The pair step into a wooden gondola that sways them down into the courtyard like a bucket into a well, stopping only centimetres above the flagstones. Teenah hops out and runs to hug Briony warmly. Mrs. Moore turns aside.

Kurd kisses Briony on both cheeks. "We were among the first to disembark from the *Emerald Tranquility*."

"It's so nice here," Teenah chirps, "like a TV reality-show set. Who shall we vote off the island first?"

"I hope it's not me," Gigot says.

Kurd wraps his arms round Gigot's lean body. "Never! You, Gigot, are indispensable."

"Frank will meet us for cocktails before dinner," Gigot informs them. "But first perhaps you wish to see the other passengers."

"A very good idea," Mrs. Moore says as they trail Gigot across the courtyard.

"Most are found in the infirmary," he says.

"So many are ill?" Teenah asks, as though she has witnessed nothing over the past few days.

"Not so ill." Gigot turns to Briony. "What's this English word for not enough water so you shiver like old fruits?"

"Shrivel?"

"Ah, sorry."

"Dehydration."

"Yes! Many are shivered up. But not so grave. We inflate them with sugar water. Here we are."

He points to a white stucco warehouse, with the metal shutters of its bays rolled up. Within each bay, passengers sit or recline in immaculate white beds. Mrs. Nightingale "Nighty" Sweeney, whom Briony hasn't seen since she barged her around at tango class, looks robust as ever. Maybelle Clabbers of the Boston Clabbers, sprightly in a silver-spangled bed jacket, Queen-waves to them. Harry Templeton, the notorious arbitrageur, smokes a cigar-sized blunt. Viscount and Viscountess Grimsley-Arserton lie thin and leathery in adjoining beds, IV lines pouring colourless liquid into their wasted arms.

Little Buddha bustles up, looking anxious. "Ah good, you're here to see my poor Mimi. Please come." He crosses his arms to block Teenah and Kurd. "Only Briony and Mrs. Moore, please."

They follow him through a low door into a darkened room, its jalousies closed. An overhead fan stirs the stale air. Rigid on a white bed, eyes bulging and moist, her gold chiffon nightgown damp with sweat, Mimi looks like her own shade.

"See who I've brought you, Mimi, my darling."

Her eyes grow larger still. "Who? *Who?*"

Little Buddha urges them toward the foot of the bed. "Your very dear friends, Briony and Mrs. Moore."

"Little B, no! Not without my —" She gestures toward the bed stand.

He retrieves the green pennant with its kissing seahorses. "Here you are, my lovely."

Mimi swings the *Emerald Tranquility* colours back and forth in a metronomic manner as her mouth forms a rictus grin. "'Your home away from home is better than home,'" she rasps. "'Embark on a journey of exotic grandeur.'"

"You see," Little Buddha says, "she almost becomes herself again."

The pennant thrashes the air as her voice grows harsher. "'Sanctuaries of welcoming comfort!'" she screams. "'Pamper yourself at the Feng Shui Spa!'"

Little Buddha moves to take the pennant from her, but she slashes him across the face with it — a crimson line slants down one cheek.

"Ladies, ladies," he says to Briony and Mrs. Moore, "So kind of you to visit. Mimi's a little overtired now. Tomorrow you'll surely find her even better improved."

"'ALL-INCLUSIVE PREMIUM SPIRITS AND SPECIALTY COFFEES!'" Mimi screeches.

Little Buddha takes their hands in his soft ones. "Please come again. You do her a world of good."

"TELL ME," MRS. MOORE says as Frank Joy tops up her glass, "how did you end up in the piracy field?"

They sit at a long table under the stars, along with those passengers still ambulatory. Gigot's also asked a number of his pirate chums to join them.

Frank Joy laughs uproariously, lustily, out of all proportion to Mrs. Moore's simple query, as if compelled to play up his piratical nature while at the same time denying it. "I'm no pirate, madame. That's a fantasy of Little Gigot's."

Gigot grins vapidly from the foot of the table.

"I'm simply an imaginative entrepreneur harnessing the bounties of the sea — for my own benefit, of course, but also for the commonweal of Yomia."

"A pirate through and through then," Mrs. Moore says.

Frank Joy laughs again, less uproariously.

"I notice you, unlike the rest of your comrades, are not French. How did you come to band together?" Kurd asks in a dreamy voice, mesmerized by Frank Joy's bare chest and shining nipples.

"Ah, is this the part of the film where I slow the action down by twirling my moustache and rolling out my dastardly backstory?"

"In the movie of your life," Teenah asks, "who would play you?"

He doesn't have to think. "Uma Thurman."

"*Chapeau!*" Gigot cries out.

"*Chapeau!*" the other pirates echo him.

"Why are they shouting about hats?" Teenah asks Briony.

"It's like 'bravo!' or 'well done!'"

"Hats off!" Gigot explains.

The pirate to his left doffs his pearl-trimmed beret.

"I stumbled on these handsome fellows at a particularly sultry hammam in Bandar seri Begawan," Frank Joy continues. "They were running their own hedonistic band of brigands out of Brunei, living haphazardly, raiding ships only when they needed money or material necessities — food, alcohol, drugs, lube, large wristwatches. They lacked organization and foresight."

"We were not so bad before, Frank Joy," a pirate with a bleeding heart tattooed on one rounded pectoral says. "We had very much *joie de vivre!*"

"*Vive la jouissance!*" his hearty mates cry out.

Teenah looks confused.

"Long live orgasms," Briony murmurs.

"You were little more than petty thieves," Mrs. Moore points out, "slipping onto a vessel to take cash and jewellery and scurry away."

"What we did first time we raided the *Emerald Tranquility*, where so much of our comrades lost their heads," a pirate wearing a quantity of purple eye shadow points out.

"I'm grateful you made that small foray." — Frank Joy raises his glass to Gigot, who squirms ecstatically in his chair — "Look at the treasure you brought me."

The pirates cheer.

"That aborted assault showed the need for more careful oversight. Besides, the real bounty of our seas is in the ships themselves and not a few gaudy trinkets."

"You don't worry you'll be caught?" Teenah asks.

"By whom? Yomia lies in disputed waters and is so small and obscure an island no one cares what we do."

Mrs. Moore leans forward in her chair. "But with so many rich Westerners in your custody, don't you fear their governments will intervene?"

"You're very shrewd, Mrs. Moore." Frank Joy bows to her and drinks deeply from his glass. "We're not so different, you and I — both of us chasing after utopias. Except mine succeeded and yours — well, here you are, my esteemed guest. In any case, do you really think the First World will —"

The great bronze gates swing open and a rickety school bus with Thai lettering on the side drives up almost to the long banquet table. Four men wearing XXL satin basketball shorts branded down the side with appliqué letters spelling out LACKERS step down, AK-47s at the ready. Not nearly so stylish or compact, Briony thinks, as the Micro-Uzis our Gummis and then our mutineers brandished.

One of the men hurries up to Frank Joy and whispers in his ear.

He leaps from his chair. "Please excuse me, ladies and gentlemen, but an urgent matter has come up that I must attend to at once."

"Even before pudding?" Gigot looks downcast.

"You will come with me, Little Gigot." He turns to Mrs. Moore and Briony. "Ladies, I'd like you to come along as well. See how we on Yomia deal with unanticipated events."

"What's happened?" Mrs. Moore asks.

"Just the tiniest renegade action," Frank Joy says. "We will have it quelled in no time."

Teenah, Kurd, and the rest of the pirates make to rise from the table. "No, no," Frank Joy says, "only Mrs. Moore and Briony are needed. Please stay and enjoy your *île flottante*."

They follow the armed men onto the bus, which smells of curry, durian, and a strange noxious odour emanating from the men themselves.

"What's that scent they're wearing?" Briony asks Gigot, who sprawls in the seat behind her and Mrs. Moore. Frank Joy's up front, conferring with his men.

"Tom Ford, *Patchouli Putain,* from a yacht we captured. You smell *le romarin* — the rosemary?"

Briony cranks down her window. "I smell dead civet cat."

Gigot opens his too. "Smell the night air, Briony. Very better."

She inhales. "Jasmine?"

"This come from the flower of the pong pong tree. Nice from very far but too close, *crise cardiaque.*" He sits back in his seat.

Mrs. Moore takes Briony's hand. "He's talking nonsense. Only the fruit itself causes heart failure."

"How do we get the fuck out of here?" Briony whispers.

"We must wait, find our time."

"By then we'll be dead."

"Thank you for your optimism, dear Briony. Aren't we both still very much alive?"

"Aren't we both still very much under house arrest?"

"We've only just arrived. First, we see how this place works, then we organize."

Gigot leans forward in his seat. "Ah, you ladies, always the love."

"You bet," Briony says as the bus emerges from the suicide-tree forest, a flood-lit compound straight ahead. As they reach the chain-link perimeter, she makes out hundreds of figures kneeling together, close-cropped heads veloured as mushroom caps.

"Why are these people praying?" Mrs. Moore calls out to Frank Joy. "Is this some sort of cult?"

"They only kneel, Mrs. Moore. Although some may be praying also."

The bus shambles to a halt at the compound gate and they all step off. As they proceed through the gate under the watchful eyes of guards who look more like plain thugs than pirates, Briony sees that the kneelers' hands are secured behind their backs. Frank Joy wades in among them, and they attempt to scuttle this way and that to avoid being trod on. "Behold, ladies, the former crew of the *Emerald Tranquility*."

Bereft of both hair and raggedy costumes, they're unrecognizable.

"But you must release them at once!" Mrs. Moore commands.

"Very soon, I promise you. This is simply a precautionary measure so we can weed out the ruffians."

"These people are unarmed. What harm can they do to you or your men?"

"Please come with me and I'll illustrate the problems we face."

Mrs. Moore and Briony tiptoe among the bound figures as Frank Joy leads the way to an open-sided hangar.

"This is an old airfield," Briony says to Mrs. Moore.

"I see no planes."

"*Oye!*" a figure at her feet cries out. "You step on my foot, silly bitch."

"Luis!" Briony says.

"Who other?" he mutters.

"Oh my god, Luis. What —"

A guard following close behind kicks Luis twice, once in the face, once in the groin. He curls into himself, whimpering.

"What the fuck?" Briony turns on the guard, but he wrenches her arm behind her before she can wrench his eyeballs from their sockets and lock-steps her into the hangar.

Another guard seizes Mrs. Moore by the arm. "Mr. Joy!" Mrs. Moore calls out, "please help us, Mr. Joy."

But he and Gigot have moved so far ahead he can't or won't hear. At the far end of the hangar, a gaggle of tiny women in pink smocks cluster in front of a low platform set with folding chairs. A wizened woman with tumultuous blond hair sits on one of the chairs. Her pink flowered wrapper nearly swallows her. Behind her, Anna May Wang holds a large pair of scissors to the older woman's throat. Behind Anna May, half a dozen guards aim their guns at the back of her head.

"Mother," Frank Joy calls out, "we're here!"

"Mama Joy!" Gigot cries.

"You come more close," Anna May shouts, "I kill your mama."

"One moment, please, Ms. Wang. Everything will be all right." Frank Joy halts at platform edge. "Mama, are you all right?"

"Do I look all right?"

"Mrs. Moore" — Frank Joy holds out his hand to her — "won't you please join us?"

"I'm afraid I'm unable to move."

Frank Joy rushes over and cuffs Mrs. Moore's guard across the face. "You must forgive me, Mrs. Moore. Sometimes my men can be a bit overzealous." At a sign from Frank Joy, the guard twisting Briony's arm relents.

"I am so very sorry, Briony." Frank Joy examines her arm. "You are unhurt?" She nods. He turns back to Mrs. Moore. "You will help me, please? Ms. Wang would kill my dear mama."

Mrs. Moore surveys the scene calmly. "How did this happen?"

"Mama was supervising haircuts for the *Emerald Tranquility* crew, and somehow Ms. Wang procured a pair of scissors. Could you please try to reason with her?"

Mrs. Moore shakes her head. "First you must bid your men to put down their weapons." Frank Joy makes a motion, and the guards behind Anna May and Mama Joy lower their assault rifles and step down from the platform. "Very good," Mrs. Moore says. "I will help your mother now, but only if you agree to help me."

"Frankie!" Mama Joy wails.

"You must tell your men to unshackle the crew."

"There are no shackles, my dear lady, only heavy-duty garbage-bag ties."

"Have them cut off."

"But of course. Once we're done here."

Mrs. Moore steps onto the platform. "Anna May! Anna May!"

"Esmiss Esmoor!" Without loosening her grip on the scissors at Mama Joy's throat, Anna May beams at Mrs. Moore.

"You must put the scissors down, Anna May."

"First I kill Mama."

"No, Anna May, you mustn't do that."

"Why not?"

"That will only make matters worse."

"Matters already worse," Anna May mutters.

"Give me the scissors, and you and I will go out of this place and address our people."

"What we will say?"

"I'll think of something. You know me, Anna May."

"Tired of talk."

"If you can talk, you're still alive."

Anna May thinks this over, nods her agreement. "Thank you, Anna May."

Anna May still holds the scissors. "I cut off Mama's ear only. Souvenir." Mama Joy howls.

"It's all right, Mama," her son urges.

"Please give me the scissors, Anna May, and then we'll go talk to our comrades."

Mrs. Moore turns to Frank Joy: "And there will be no reprisals of any kind against Ms. Wang."

"Why should I agree to that?"

The older woman goes eye to eye with him. "Because if you don't, I'll turn Anna May loose on your mother's carotid artery.

Frank Joy scowls at her. "Fine."

"Anna May." Mrs. Moore holds out her hand. *"Please."*

Anna May relinquishes the scissors, and Mama Joy slides to the floor. A guard rushes forward to seize Anna May, who quivers with adrenalin, but Frank Joy and Gigot leap to the stage. Gigot steps between the guard and Anna May while Frank Joy tries to calm his furious mother.

Anna May, Mrs. Moore, and Briony walk out into the floodlit glare. Guards make their way among the prone workers, snipping off their plastic manacles. Once they are on their feet, swaying and tilting as if the night wind buffets them, Anna May throws up her arms and cries, "Esmiss Esmoor! Esmiss Esmoor! Here! Now! Now! Here!"

Staggered by the bright artificial light, their individuality effaced by their new and merciless haircuts and shapeless grey pyjamas, the crew look more bewildered than anything. Some lick their lips compulsively, others are unable to stand still, their bare feet slapping against the tarmac, fingers pattering relentlessly on their own upturned faces. Frank Joy and Gigot stand to one side, grinning broadly at their antics.

"Drugged," Mrs. Moore whispers to Briony. "He's had them all drugged."

The old woman steps forward and they billow about her, grimacing and fidgeting, dancing and pogo-ing, fluttering their fingers in her face. It's not clear to Briony they know who Mrs. Moore is, but they're glad to see her nevertheless. "My friends," she begins, but is unable to continue as tears stream from her eyes. The crew close in round her and stroke her cheeks softly with their fingertips. More restless hands pat her all over, as though she is an aged baby they would soothe. From their mouths emerge ghostly sighs. They swirl away with her. Briony tracks her progress only by glimpses of her shining hair, the bright amethyst grapes. This encompassing, jittery, susurrating dance whirls on and on. Taking it all in, Frank Joy looks alarmed. Briony thinks it must be as clear to him as it is to her that their sighs and whispers are screams they're unable to voice.

Eventually he signals the guards to extricate Mrs. Moore from the dervish throng. They pull her out, pale and stricken.

"We must return to the compound now," Frank Joy

explains to her. She stares blindly past him. "To have our pudding."

As they reach the gates, Briony turns and yells, "Luis! Where are you, Luis?"

Frank Joy claps a big warm hand over her mouth. "Who the fuck's Luis?"

"A friend of mine."

"You don't even know he's here."

"I saw him. Earlier. He tried to say something but one of your goons beat him."

"My guards are instructed to use the least amount of force possible while maintaining absolute control."

"Right." Briony screams once more before he can stop her. "LUIS!"

He slaps her so hard it jars her brain.

"Frank!" Gigot shouts. "What do you do?"

Frank Joy shoves her into a nearby guard's arms and turns to Gigot. "Watch out, *petite salope,* or I'll do it to you too."

"I am no slut," Gigot says. "Not now I'm with you."

"Once a slut, always a slut!" Frank Joy stalks away.

"He does not mean this," Gigot says to Briony as the guard hustles her onto the bus. "He has only the angry management issues." He closely inspects her throbbing cheek. "Sometimes his fury carries him away."

"Never mind. What about my friend Luis? Can you find out about him?"

"If guards were mean to him he'll convalesce in the infirmary."

"Back at the compound?"

"No, camp infirmary. He will be fined."

"'Fine'?"

"That too."

Briony sits down next to a stunned Mrs. Moore, who's unaware of her presence. Frank Joy comes aboard, his face a dark study. He sits down next to Gigot, who turns to stare out the window into the deep-blue night.

BRIONY WAKES IN THE middle of the night to find Mrs. Moore sitting at the foot of her bed. "Forgive my intrusion."

"When we returned to the compound, I asked you to stay with me — I guess you didn't hear me," Briony says.

"No, I didn't. I fear this has often been the case, hearing only my own voice."

"Sometimes the case, yes. Don't exaggerate."

"You're too kind. It's all my fault."

"What is?"

Mrs. Moore's hand sweeps the darkened room. "All this. A successful mutiny ending in disaster, the crew's internment in a camp."

"You couldn't have known it would end this way."

"I ignored my own inner voice, back on the ship. The one that said, 'If you liberate the crew, what will happen to them?' In unbottling their rage, I have brought the Furies down on them. How did I think their action wouldn't end in reaction? Why didn't I think to prepare them for this?

"What's happened here could have been predicted, in both its force and proportion. It might have been avoided, had it not been for an old woman's ego, her white woman's dream of emancipation, her white woman's weightless burden."

"But chastising yourself so — what good does it do?"

"It does no good at all, and yet it's still all my fault."

"The pirates overpowered us. They have more firepower and are better organized for this kind of thing. They kidnapped us and brought us here. That's all."

"That's not all. It might have ended with Navy SEALS crashing in to save the hostages while killing half of them, or some Asian state claiming their territory and efficiently disappearing us all. Instead we have Frank Joy and his mob. I've left the workers far more powerless than they were before. This is a terrible sin."

Briony searches out her eyes, but Mrs. Moore turns her face to the wall. "You think it's all over? We'll be stranded here forever?" Briony asks.

"Oh, the passengers — they may end up ransomed, should they survive until then. The *Emerald Tranquility* crew — who would bother to ransom them? And how to differentiate them from all the other slaves on the island? You've seen the rendering yards — how long will any of them last, now he has drugged them into submission?"

"There must be something we can do."

Mrs. Moore finds her eyes. "Oh, dear Briony, I never had you down for an optimist."

"I'm just a starry-eyed fool — I always thought you'd come to love me too."

Her dry laugh. "Maybe you're not so starry-eyed."

"No?"

"You won that battle long ago, when you cried before me over my failure to love you."

"Then why couldn't you have —"

"— said something? Taken you in my arms? Because I'm in no way worthy of anyone's love, least of all yours. I'm guilty of negligence on so many levels — toward the workers, toward you."

Briony, drowning in sadness, doesn't know what to say.

She draws back the sheet. "Please, Mrs. Moore. You look so — so pale and —"

"Old? You may say it."

"Tired, I was going to say 'tired.' You need sleep."

"I'm past sleeping."

Briony holds out her arms. "Come to bed."

"Why?"

"So I can hold you. So I can console you, though this is new to me and may prove awkward."

"I don't deserve to be consoled."

"Everyone deserves that."

"Even you, my dear?"

"Let's worry about me later."

"'Love is not consolation. Love is light.' I forget who said that."

She stands unsteadily and bends her face to Briony's. "Good night, my love."

Her lips brush Briony's, and she slips out the door.

"THIS MELON AND PASSION FRUIT smoothie is divine."
Teenah pats Frank Joy's big hand.

"Indeed," Kurd says. Right on point, Briony thinks.
Only pseuds say "indeed." Or "on point," to be fair.

The long breakfast table is more populated than the
previous night. Mrs. Nightingale "Nighty" Sweeney
chats amiably with Gigot, while Harry Templeton and
Count Guido Malodoroso untangle Viscountess Grimsley-
Arserton's IV line as the Viscount smooths a napkin
across her lap. At the far end, Mrs. Spitz-Basenji feeds
toast points laden with caviar, crème fraîche, and chives
to her unkempt little Pomeranian as Mama Joy looks on,
appalled.

"You promised us a full tour of the island," Teenah
says teasingly.

"Did I?" Frank Joy asks.

"Indeed," Kurd says. Briony feels she may gouge out
his eyes with a grapefruit spoon.

"You've already seen most of it."

"Only in passing." Mrs. Moore looks combative.

"Our little island's not that interesting, I'm afraid."

"Come now, Mr. Joy. We found the camp last night
most interesting." Mrs. Moore holds out her demitasse
for a guard to refill it.

"Oh yes?" Teenah says. "How was it?"

"Don't you think everyone should see, Mr. Joy?"

"There's not much left to see, Mrs. Moore. We emptied the camp this morning."

"Did you?"

"Yes, except for a few who require further remediation."

"Cramming them with more drugs, are you?"

Frank Joy lets loose a devilish laugh.

"Surely there are better ways to keep them in line."

He reaches across the table to touch Mrs. Moore's hand. "Would you prefer they be tortured?"

She pulls her hand away. "I would prefer they be free."

"Freedom's such a relative thing here on the island."

"You think I haven't noticed?"

"After we were so gentle with your Anna May Wang, she and some of her friends escaped the compound during the night."

"Oh?" Mrs. Moore's face brightens.

Frank Joy pushes his abundant curls behind his ears. "A momentary inconvenience. We will have them back soon and will deal with them our way."

Count Guido Malodoroso rises from the table, tattered burgundy dressing gown flapping about stick legs. "I for one would like to bathe in the sea."

"Hear! Hear!" Harry Templeton flicks a speck of dirt off his nearly immaculate white driving shoes. "Most refreshing."

"You will all die," Mama Joy says. Briony wonders at the woman's characteristic tact.

"Dear lady," Harry Templeton says, "I hardly think

this a hospitable way to address us—we are your guests."

"You're our prisoners," Mama Joy says. "No pretending you're not. Anyway, the sea here's so polluted you can walk on it."

"I'm afraid Mama's right. The beaches could do with a bit of a cleanup too. Our environmental reclamation program's still in its infancy," Frank Joy says.

"If the crew are no longer at the camp," Briony asks, "where have you taken them?"

Frank Joy looks very pleased with himself. "To the ship-breaking yards, to put them to work. If that goes well, we'll have them in suitable housing by nightfall. They've already had a hearty breakfast, not entirely different from your own."

"Oh?"

"Powdered eggs and turkey bacon—the same breakfast they had on the *Emerald Tranquility*, I believe." Frank Joy laughs. "That's where we got it."

"Perhaps we could go view their work, offer some words of encouragement," Mrs. Moore says. "Last night I was so moved by their plight I couldn't speak."

"This could be arranged." He looks down the table at the other passengers. It's clear to Briony that the Grimsley-Arsertons are in no shape to go anywhere, but, ever game, Mrs. Nightingale "Nighty" Sweeney, Maybelle Clabbers, Harry Templeton, Count Guido Malodoroso, and Mrs. Spitz-Basenji announce themselves delighted at the prospect of an excursion.

"Will there be shops?" Maybelle Clabbers asks.

. . .

A DUBIOUS-LOOKING, GLEAMING LIQUID trickles along fissures in the ship-breaking yard's sand as barefoot workers drag sections of metal piping out of the yawning hull of a partially dismembered tanker with "KINGFISH R" painted on its bow. On the lookout for Luis, Briony tries to distinguish one crew member from another, but their grey pyjamas and stubbled heads make this impossible. Where, she wonders, have Anna May, Evangelista, Tuk-Tuk, Mercedes, Darna, Choum, Chit, and Izz gone?

"Don't step too close, ladies," Frank Joy warns, "I wouldn't want you to ruin your pretty shoes."

"Or your pretty feet," Gigot adds.

Teenah tiptoes across the polychrome sand, her gold gladiator sandals looking particularly inappropriate to Briony — though where outside a Las Vegas coliseum would such footwear *be* appropriate? The Cuban heels and soles of Kurd's patent-leather biker boots are already as bronzed as memento baby shoes.

As they follow Frank Joy toward a section of the yards lined with feeble palms, where workers pry motherboards out of cracked-open computers, Mrs. Moore whispers to Briony: "I will distract Mr. Joy and you can ask the crew about Anna May and your friend Luis."

Briony feigns passionate interest in the complex skein of wiring a team of young women attempt to untangle as Mrs. Moore approaches Frank Joy.

Trying not to move her lips, Briony proves to be a poor ventriloquist. "I'm trying to find —"

"Why you talk funny?" one of the women says straight out, slurring her own words.

"Shh! I'm trying to find Luis."

"Who is Luis?

"His shipboard name was Collins—he was my butler."

Another woman looks up from the tangled wires. "Fancy-fancy."

"Where *you* stay?" a third, blank-eyed woman demands, studying Briony's spotless attire. "Not with us, for sure."

"Or Anna May?" Briony tries again, "has anyone seen Anna May?"

Their heads go down and they begin to slowly sway from side to side. "Don't say her name. Never say her name." One of them adds, "Bugger off, chop-chop."

"I'm trying to help!"

"Yeah, yeah. Everyone help so much." With their heads down, Briony can't tell who's saying what. "Fuck off, rich bitch."

"Briony!" Gigot calls back to her. "Please stay with the group—is very dangerous place."

She hurries to catch up with the others. "Sorry," she says to Frank Joy. "Who knew there were so many parts to a ship?"

He regards her with suspicion. "There will be time for fraternization later, when they've settled into their quarters."

"They all work so hard in the hot sun." Mrs. Spitz-Basenji looks up at Frank Joy's beautiful, pitiless face. "Shouldn't they at least have water bottles and small tubes of sunscreen?"

"Soon," Gigot says, "very soon!"

"And sandals," Harry Templeton throws in. "Get them all some good sturdy sandals, man! It will pay off in terms of team efficiency and reduce future medical costs."

A bell clangs in the distance. Women with veiled faces and begrimed saris arrive, pushing wheelbarrows that clink with silver canisters.

"Tiffin!" they call out, "time for tiffin!"

Workers converge from across the rendering yards, some in civilian clothes, the crew members in uniform grey.

As the tiffin lids come off, Mrs. Nightingale "Nighty" Sweeney lifts her nose to sniff the breeze. "Eww!"

"Durian mash with lime and green chilies," Frank Joy says. "It has a slightly fecal odour but is delicious to taste, I'm told, though it's said to repeat fiercely. Easy to harvest and store too."

"Mr. Joy?" Mrs. Moore touches his sinewy arm.

"Yes?"

"With everyone pausing for lunch, I wonder if I might be allowed, now my wits are more about me, to address the *Emerald Tranquility* crew? They have been through so much."

He turns to face her. Roughly the same height, they stand eye to eye. "Nothing seditious?" he asks.

"Nothing remotely seditious, Mr. Joy. I promise you."

He steps forward, expecting Mrs. Moore to move back: they collide, bumping noses.

"Ow!" Frank Joy cries — a bead of blood slides from his left nostril. The more hard-headed of the two, Mrs. Moore says nothing.

"I have one request." Frank Joy breaks their standoff while dabbing at his nose with his fingertips.

"Yes?"

"During your address, could you add a word or two — perhaps in the peroration — about the importance of settling peacefully into their new jobs and co-operating with the authorities? It will make life here so much easier for everyone."

"'Peroration'? I do admire a man with a vocabulary. Where did you go to school?"

"I was a Rhodes Scholar in my youth."

"Of course you were — I can see it now. You're not at all unlike dear Cecil himself. He kept workers in camps too." She reaches out to touch his cheek. He flinches. "Why, you're hardly more than a boy. Or should I say a Boy Scout, what with all your little adventures? I will tell them whatever you think will make things run more smoothly."

"I trust you," he says, "almost implicitly."

Mrs. Moore smiles. "Isn't that the best any of us can do?"

He cups his hands. "Listen up, people! Could the former crew of the *Emerald Tranquility* come forward? Mrs. Moore would like to say a few words to you."

Much commotion among the workers, along with a strange low throbbing like cicadas pulsing on a hot afternoon as the crew push their way to the fore. A line of guards step forward to keep them from getting too close to either Mrs. Moore or Frank Joy.

"My friends," Mrs. Moore begins, "last night in the camp I was so overwhelmed I was unable to speak." The cicada pulsing becomes a heaving wave of sound rising from deep within the workers. Their eyes are glassy, pupils dilated. Still drugged then, Briony thinks, and heavy-limbed.

"My very dear friends," Mrs. Moore begins again. "To see you here causes an old woman's heart to break. Even before our travels together began, you had all come from so far away on your own separate voyages from so many nations, from countries with too many people and not enough to eat, leaving all those you loved behind — wives leaving husbands, husbands wives, young parents leaving small children, older children leaving parents and grand-parents. What a tremendous, painful risk you undertook.

"Once aboard the *Emerald Tranquility*, you worked so long and hard and tirelessly for so little money — though more than you'd ever have made at home — much of which you sent back to the families you loved and hun-gered for, while receiving little gratitude from those you served onboard that luxurious ship. To them you were all the same — of a lower caste, darker-skinned than them-selves, interchangeable.

"I know, because so many of you have told me, that you wept in your narrow bunks at night, out of sadness, fatigue, and yes, even despair. How far can you stretch the bonds of love without sundering them? Yet you always had time to console one another, to look out for your friends and fellow workers even when you had so little free time of your own."

The cicada sound has become a weird invasive trilling that shreds the granular air.

"On my first few voyages I merely observed. When we did finally make contact, I learned of your deepest longings, your highest aspirations. Stories of your hopes and dreams, your losses and regrets, touched me as nothing ever had before. I determined to help you, in any way I could, to achieve your dreams of a better life, a more equal one."

Frank Joy steps closer to Mrs. Moore, touching her shoulder to warn her off this bothersome topic. But at his touch, she sinks to her knees in a rush of white linen, like a great bird alighting.

"I must apologize to you all, to all my friends, for leading you in the wrong direction, for leaving you worse off, far worse off" — she looks about her at the despoiled beach, the dismembered ships, the thin and wavering workers— "than you were before. Because I was so intoxicated by your seizure of power, I failed to concern myself with the consequences. At some level it all remained only a delightful game to me, to see you briefly and boldly so free and joyous, without thinking of how to protect you from the coming storm."

Frank Joy attempts to draw her to her feet, but she shakes him off. The incessant shrieking insect sounds of the crew crescendo into a seismic, wordless chant, fuelled by rage, while their eyes remain opaque, lifeless.

"Frank Joy has asked me to urge you to co-operate with his regime. But this I cannot bring myself to do."

Frank Joy motions for a pair of guards to seize Mrs. Moore, but Briony steps between them and the kneeling old woman.

"What I can urge," Mrs. Moore continues, unheeding, "is that you maintain your solidarity, your mighty allegiance to one another and to a more just and righteous world. And I must, after so many irresponsible half-truths and lies, tell you frankly that whatever you do will be insignificant against the powers that oppress you, but it is crucial nevertheless that you do it, for there lies your strength, there your —"

The guards throw Briony aside and drag Mrs. Moore away, her feet trailing in the foul sand.

The air becomes alive and deadly as silver discs flash, spinning across the sky. The tiffin women have thrown off their veils: Briony watches as Anna May launches a lid that slices open Frank Joy's cheek. He puts his hand to the opening wound: rivulets of blood pour between his fingers. Anna May, Evangelista, Tuk-Tuk, Mercedes, Darna, Choum, Chit, and Izz must have filed down the lids to razor sharpness. They catch the panicking guards' foreheads, noses, chins — Briony sees one bright disc cleanly separate one guard's ear from his head.

The guards not busy mopping their bloody faces raise their assault rifles in one practised movement. A deafening barrage cuts the arcing swirl of silver lids: saris bloom crimson. Other crew members collapse around them, pyjamas darkening as they fall.

Mrs. Moore tears free from her guards and wheels round to cry, "Briony, watch out!" as a wayward disc whirls past her nose. One of the guards brings down the butt of his rifle on the back of Mrs. Moore's head with a sodden crunching blow. She sways a moment, upright in the echoing air, before coming down slowly to land face-down in the sand.

At her side without knowing how she got there, Briony can't find purchase in the matted silver hair, the tiny amethyst shards, and the sliding gore, but she does manage to turn Mrs. Moore over so she can see her unmarred face and astonished eyes, her parted lips flecked with grains of sand.

"You've killed her!" she screams at the guard towering over her, "You've fucking killed Mrs. Moore!"

He shrugs and spits on the ground. "Just another rich old lady."

Gigot's "Briony, head up!" is the last thing she hears.

18

A LOT TO BE said for a coma. For two sunrises and one sunset, enrobed in smooth white marble, Briony plays an effigy atop her own tomb. Figures come to tap on or run their fingers over the polished surface, but translucent stone protects her from penetration.

She feels she has shared enough to date and is not about to dole out her sadness. Nobody's business if she's blue. Not that she is, exactly. What would be the point of that?

Frozen is best.

But the world refuses to leave her alone. Pain scalds her skull as the marble shears away in soundless slabs. Mama Joy stands over her, sinking a hypodermic needle again and again into her cheeks and nose.

"Ha!" she cries. "That wakes you up."

Tears spill down Briony's cheeks.

"You were out so long I didn't think you were coming back."

She tries to answer but it comes out throttled.

"What's that, honey?" Mama Joy inserts a straw between Briony's clenched teeth. Her mouth's so numb, the water she slurps leaks everywhere.

"Not long enough," she croaks. "Didn't know you were a nurse."

"Not really, but I'll have to do. Better than that old

sawbones down in the camp infirmary. Let me crank up your bed."

Not the best idea—Briony's whole body seizes up.

"Goodness, who's a sensitive plant? There's others far worse off than you."

She looks about the empty white infirmary. "Where are they?"

Mama Joy looks about blankly. "Who?"

"The sick passengers, the wounded crew."

Mama Joy pats her arm. "The passengers have all recovered, at least those who survived. The wounded workers are all down in the camp infirmary—better for them to be with their own kind, don't you think?"

"How many—?"

"Speak up."

"How many crew died, how many passengers?"

Mama Joy clucks her tongue. "Now that's not a very cheerful subject. Why would you ever want to know the unhappy total? Best for you to concentrate on you and your own self-care. Maybe you can ask Frank later? He has all the stats. A fair number of crew lost their lives in the fracas."

"Firing squad?"

"Hardly that, honey. Those people were drugged up and out of control—they had to be stopped. Yomia's an orderly place, and my boy Frankie will see it's kept that way."

"Where is he?"

"Convalescing in his suite—he received a nasty face wound, nearly as bad as yours."

"What happened to me?"

"From the look of things, I'd say the hind end of a rifle. You're lucky to be with us."

So lucky.

"What's that, hon?"

"A mirror. I'd like to see a mirror."

"Plenty of time for that, once we've removed the sutures and can get a better sense of how you're healing. The main thing is you're conscious and sitting up — back among the living."

"I'm so delighted."

"I'd think you would be, doll."

EVENING ALREADY, WHITE WALLS gone grey. Gigot stands at the foot of the bed with a rickety wheelchair. "Can you rise from bed, *ma chère* Briony?"

"Why would I want to do that?"

"Pompes funèbres."

"Funeral rites? Do I look that bad?"

"No, no — for the victims."

"Where?"

"At camp. Big deal. Everyone there, all dead."

She's about to swing her legs out of bed when her skull cracks in two and she groans accordingly.

"*Tiens*, Briony." He taps two gold capsules into her quaking palm. "Under the tongue — you will feel so better."

He lifts her from the bed. How his naked torso warms her until the pain puts her out again.

She wakes up in the speeding jeep, her agony tolerable now but nowhere near gone. Ravenous chipmunks seem to be eating lettuce inside her ears.

"Gigot?"

"Yes?"

"Do you think we could go more slowly?"

"Ah, sorry, sorry. We're late already."

Dense black smoke palls the jolting jeep along with odours she recognizes from *El Supuesto Palacio de Patos Blancos* in Modigliano.

"I think we're too late, dear Briony."

In the distance, under scattered stars, a fiery mountain of scorched logs and thick tree branches, wooden beams, bedsteads and credenzas, desks and chairs, sofa frames and other less-identifiable ship furniture and fixtures. Interleaved among the detritus, fast-flaming bodies that twist and shudder and curl in upon themselves like blackened fetuses as the conflagration consumes them. How many bodies, she can't tell—the tarmac's too thronged with mourners, and Gigot's unable to drive much beyond the camp gate. But scores, she's sure. More than scores. Sizzling noises reach her as melting fat drips into the fire, the skulls and bones revealed amid terrible liquification, and finally bodies and bones above collapsing onto bodies and bones below as the mountain shifts and heaves and thinner wood burns and falls away until only charred tree trunks angle through the ash-speckled heat.

Mourners surge this way and that, chanting, the words unintelligible over the crackling flames. Are they still drugged? Briony wonders, still speechless?

A procession of men and women, all naked and smeared with white ash, wind their way through the throngs, carrying high on their bare shoulders a long pale package: Mrs. Moore wrapped in her own bloodstained linen, her face covered by a square of gold silk. They ease her onto the slowly subsiding mountain. The silk flames first and, before the fire devours her, Briony glimpses her sharp profile.

The naked women who have accompanied Mrs. Moore to the pyre continue their chanting. At first just random sounds, but gradually they resolve into four clear syllables: "ESMISS ESMOOR! ESMISS ESMOOR! ESMISS ESMOOR!"

She makes out Anna May in the middle of the naked throng, her head wrapped in bloodied gauze. Briony joins in the chanting, though it hurts her mouth to open so wide:

"Esmiss Esmoor!"

Now only her bones, brightening through the inferno. Esmiss Esmoor, Esmiss Esmoor.

BRIONY FEELS SHE HAS little to complain of — a want of freedom perhaps, but really at this point, her fucks cupboard is bare. The island now another ship, different but still becalmed. Up here in the compound, she lacks for nothing. Down in the camp, where a few malcontents remain for re-education, or in the new circle of clapped-together housing where recanting crew members now reside, all same-same, as the wise man said: long sun-stained hours, wracking labour, foul accidents, sudden death—a rare day when one comes without the other. Nothing new except the abrupt descent from low pay to no pay. Apart from the occasional drive-by on the way to somewhere else, *Emerald Tranquility* passengers aren't allowed to visit the camp or the raw new housing. One time she thought she saw Luis's angry eyes glaring out from a work detail hauling the screw from an enormous engine along the beach. Most likely wishful thinking.

She knows she could arrange to go down to the rendering yards on carefully escorted visits, but what would she do there? She has no capabilities that would help the workers. Would she set up a school to teach the children the tenets of luxury journalism? With her recently reconfigured face, she wonders if she might retrain as a clown and entertain the troops.

She's too tired to fight, and anyway no enemy's present. Frank Joy's still incommunicado in his penthouse suite. Although Mama Joy gives daily reports on how well he's rallying, Gigot and the other pirates sing a more mournful tune detailing infection, disorientation, mad rages, weeping fits.

In his absence, discipline has gone slack: the guards inebriated by mid-afternoon, orgiastic rustling in the bamboo plantations, the compound gates left unlocked. She could escape easily, but where would she go? Join Anna May and her shrinking band of guerrillas in the mountains?

Much of the time, she sits on her high balcony and watches the meaningless activities of her fellow passengers. As on any cruise ship, everything revolves around meals. The quality of food remains high, though one does tire after a time of suckling pig or truffles sprinkled on every goddamn thing.

Most of the time her appetite's low to non-existent, so she doesn't often go down for First or even Second Seating. A handful of macadamia nuts and a cube-cut papaya more than sustain her. Sometimes the others pause in their mastications to salute or toast her, high on her perch.

Last night Count Guido Malodoroso serenaded her in his tatterdemalion dressing gown, but she couldn't make out either the tune or the words. Music means nothing to her now — more grating than anything else, a lot of effort expended for a few random squeaks.

For the others, she knows boredom's a problem. Teenah and Kurd are dying of it; Teenah showed up at breakfast this morning in *sweatpants*, for god's sake. Viscount Grimsley-Arserton wanders about the courtyard or rides the bucket elevator up and down, chatting away with the Viscountess, now long departed. On the brighter side, Harry Templeton and Mrs. Spitz-Basenji have moved in together, a circumstance depressed little Mrs. Miniver has taken hard.

She hasn't seen much of Little Buddha lately. How thin he has become — hard to believe she once called him Little Butter. Gigot told her he mostly stays in his single-occupancy stateroom, meditating and mourning.

What's to meditate? she wonders. Their world has ended and they're still here.

. . .

MIDDLE OF THE THROBBING NIGHT. Gigot hovers over her.

He holds a finger to her lips and motions for her to follow him. She rummages about on the floor for something to wear.

She sleeps in Mrs. Moore's oldest linen shift, wrinkled as an accordion now, but she'll never send it to the laundry, not with her scent still on it.

"No time," he whispers. "You are fine."

She heads automatically for the elevator bucket, but he signals they should take the rackety emergency ladders down. They tiptoe across the moon-washed courtyard, past a trio of guards snoring on the flagstones.

Mrs. Nightingale "Nighty" Sweeney, Maybelle Clabbers, Harry Templeton, Mrs. Spitz-Basenji, and Count Guido Malodoroso are already crammed into the ancient jeep. Nighty pats the seat next to her, flashes Briony a lubricious smile.

"Where are we going?" she asks Gigot as he climbs into the driver's seat.

His eyes glow enormous in the dark. "Escape!"

"But what about Frank?"

"I kill him, the shit."

"Mama Joy?"

"Still alive but asleep *en profondeur.*" He mimes a hypodermic sinking into his forearm. "Too scary to kill."

They drive with lights extinguished, rattling down the mountain road and past the emptied camp, leaving the desolate village, the bleak new housing, and the ship-breaking yards behind.

After climbing a rough coastal track for several

kilometres with waves sighing on their right and white-blossomed pong pong trees exhaling toxic sweetness on their left, they arrive at a narrow cove under a smoothed indigo sky.

Little Buddha awaits them, almost hidden by his saffron veils, standing next to a battered Zodiac that already contains Teenah and Kurd in matching striped Breton jerseys and spotless white ducks and, miraculously, Major Chelmsworth Cholmondeley, a wispy spectre clutching his malacca cane.

"Get in, get in," Little Buddha admonishes. "You are our last load. I have already transported four sets of passengers."

A tugboat awaits in the distance. Briony can just make its name: *Muzukashii Desu.*

She's about to join the other passengers in the Zodiac, but something makes her hesitate.

"Where are we going?"

"I tell you, Briony — we escape." Gigot no longer bothers to whisper.

"Escape to where?"

"We will steer the tugboat into a shipping channel and await to be discovered," Little Buddha says.

"I don't know —" Briony tries to gather her thoughts.

"What's to know?" Maybelle Clabbers barks. "Get in the boat!"

"But what about —" She knows she has an important question to ask but can't think what it might be.

"Come on, Briony," Teenah calls from the Zodiac. "No time to lose."

She looks up at the dark sky: Luis's raging eyes stare down at her. She remembers. "What about the crew?"

"The crew?" Mrs. Spitz-Basenji looks perplexed, as though she's never heard of such an animal.

"There isn't room for *everyone*," Nighty Nightingale says.

"The boat's full," Mrs. Spitz-Basenji adds. Mrs. Miniver yaps her approval.

"Besides," Harry Templeton says, "what did they ever do for us besides take us hostage and steal our things? I still haven't recovered my bespoke velvet smoking slippers."

"We must hurry, my little Briony," Kurd says. "Who cares about the crew?"

"Get in the fucking boat," Major Chelmsworth Cholmondeley croaks.

"I care about the crew!" Briony shouts, "And I won't leave without them!"

"Honestly, Briony," Teenah says, "now you're sounding like that crazy old lady. Anyway, there's no room for anyone else."

"Mrs. Moore wasn't crazy!"

"Oh, come on, Briony," Maybelle Clabbers says, "the old girl was completely dotty."

"Yeah," Teenah says, "bonkers."

"She wasn't crazy, and I loved her."

"Of course you did, the old dear." Teenah swats away a mosquito. "But she certainly wasn't the most stable person around."

"Urging the crew to mutiny," Harry Templeton says.

"Putting our lives in danger," Mrs. Spitz-Basenji adds.

"Get in this bloody boat, Miss Briony," Count Guido Malodoroso commands. "Enough of your nonsense."

She steps away from the Zodiac.

"Briony, *come on!*" Teenah rages.

"You can say all you want about Mrs. Moore," she tells them, "but at least she was on the right side." She turns to walk away.

Little Buddha comes stumbling up after her, grabs her arm. He's so light now it's like batting away a spent balloon.

As she climbs behind the wheel of the jeep, Gigot calls out, "But where you will go?"

"Back to the camp, the village, the ship-breaking yards."

"I wish to stay too, Briony, but the guards will kill me."

"It's okay, Gigot, I understand."

"But what will you do there?" Little Buddha asks. "What assistance can someone like you provide the poor workers?"

"She's mad, too," Briony can hear Teenah murmur to Kurd, as Gigot pushes the Zodiac into the surf.

"Whatever I do will be insignificant, but so crucial."

"What the fuck?" Teenah says.

All their confused ghostly faces bob above the black water.

Briony guns the jeep and peels out of there.

ACKNOWLEDGEMENTS

First thanks go to my friend Bruce Walsh, House of Anansi's publisher. *The Swells* marks my second book with him, and my admiration and affection have only deepened. We have become that rare thing — old queer bros strewing pixie dust wherever we go.

My usual readers and a few new ones helped with advice — thank you Anne Carson and Phoebe Fregoli — and exasperation — thank you Anne Collins and Bruce Garside. Janet Aitken, Craige Roberts, Laurence Blandford, and Lawrence Baer gave great notes and encouragement along the way.

Regarding the editing process, Gregory McCormick acted as the first, informal, and invaluable editor on *The Swells*, followed by brilliant in-house work from Joshua Greenspon, assistant editor at House of Anansi. Freelance copy editor Allegra Robinson fearlessly wrangled my errant syntax. Anansi's art director, Alysia Shewchuk, doubled and inverted Hokusai's *The Great Wave off Kanagawa* to kinetic effect, and proofreader Alison Strobel unearthed the errors all the rest of us missed.

Final thanks to E. M. Forster and Evelyn Waugh. What anxiety of influence?

Photo Credit: Justine Latour

WILL AITKEN has written three previous novels — *Realia*, *A Visit Home*, and *Terre Haute* — and the non-fiction books *Death in Venice: A Queer Film Classic* and *Antigone Undone: Juliette Binoche, Anne Carson, Ivo van Hove, and the Art of Resistance*, which was shortlisted for the Hilary Weston Writers' Trust Prize for Nonfiction. He lives in Montreal.